DOUBLE
DECEPTION

Chrissie Loveday

CHIVERS

| British Library Cataloguing in Publication Data available |

This Large Print edition published by AudioGO Ltd, Bath, 2012.
Published by arrangement with the Author

U.K. Hardcover   ISBN   978 1 4713 1483 4
U.K. Softcover   ISBN   978 1 4713 1484 1

Printed and bound in Great Britain by
MPG Books Group Limited

CHAPTER ONE

Georgie glanced out of the window. He was there again. The gorgeous young man had been hanging round the café nearly every day lately. Who was he? And why was he always there, sometimes looking out towards the sea but mostly looking at the café. Was he stalking her? If so, why? She shook her head telling herself to stop being so neurotic. How could he possibly know her real identity?

Georgie sighed as her boss, Audrey, called her to take the latest order to the table.

'Two toasted tea cakes and a pot of tea for two for table six,' Audrey said as she handed over the tray.

Her feet were aching and the backs of her legs were screaming, letting her know that she had been standing for much too long. But, she gritted her teeth, determined that she was going to stick out this job for at least the next few weeks. She was going to prove her parents were wrong about her.

She carried the tray over to the two ladies who were sitting at the window table. Georgie smiled at them.

'Thank you dear. Such a lovely spot you have here. It's a real pleasure to watch the children enjoying the beach.'

'And a lovely day for the holidaymakers,'

1

the other added.

*   *   *

'Do you want a break Gina?' Audrey asked, breaking into her thoughts. Georgie gave a slight start, still unused to her new name. 'You can take ten minutes while there's a bit of a lull.'

'Thanks. I'd love a break. I could do with a drink myself. Is there some tea left?'

She took her mug outside and sat at a spare table overlooking the beach. The little Cornish fishing village was postcard pretty and one of the few remaining places unspoilt by a plethora of conversions into holiday accommodation. It was a million miles away from the plush chain of Hetherington Hotels owned by her parents. Anyone from home who knew her would have been amazed to see her working so hard in this tiny café. She was known as a girl who revelled in going to parties, shopping and generally doing very little but enjoying herself. What exactly she had hoped to achieve by running away she couldn't say, but she was tasting independence and surviving on her own for the first time in her life.

'Hello. Enjoying a break?' She swung round, startled. It was him. She hesitated, still wondering why he was hanging around so much. His dark good looks had appealed

2

to her when she had first noticed him at a distance but now here, close up, she felt her heart pounding.

His almost green eyes stared into her own. Green? Or should it be hazel? Or were they brownish? She tried to appear casual and tried to convince herself that she should be cautious. She needed to be cautious.

He spoke again and she realised she hadn't said a word. 'I've seen you in the café several times but you always looked so busy. I wanted to come inside but it's a bit of a "ladies who lunch" sort of place. I didn't want to disturb you.'

You would disturb me any time, she thought. He was surprisingly well spoken and had a most appealing, almost boyish grin. She drew her breath and gave a weak smile, not wanting to appear too rude.

'We do get the odd few brave males venturing inside,' she said lightly.

She must look a sight, she thought. She brushed back the strand of blonde hair that had escaped from the cap she was supposed to wear for hygiene's sake. The short black skirt and bright T-shirt with a logo were hardly the most flattering clothes but, for heaven's sakes, he'd stopped for a chat, hadn't he?

'You must live around here, if you've looked into the café regularly,' she continued.

'Only been looking since you've been working there. Nearly four weeks now, isn't it?'

Despite herself, she grinned and nodded. Who was this man?

'I work at the Clarence Hotel, just up the hill. I'm on evenings this week so I have to make the most of the days. Not very good for any sort of social life.'

'I'd better go back inside soon or I'll be in trouble with the boss. Nice to talk to you.'

'Hang on a minute. I'm Jay. Jay Jacobs.' He held a hand out for her to shake. 'I'll bite the bullet and come inside one of these days.'

'Gina. Er Gina . . . Hind.'

'You don't sound exactly sure,' he teased.

'Just very weary. I'm not used to standing for so long.'

'Well, Gina Hind, maybe one of these days we'll both have time off at the same time. We could go for a drink? Or something to eat, if you like?'

'Sounds good, as long as it isn't a Cornish Cream Tea. I doubt I shall ever face eating one again after this summer. Just the smell of tea and scones might finish me off.'

Somehow, she couldn't believe he was anything more than a gorgeous man asking for a date. There was nothing about him to confirm that she needed to be cautious. He couldn't possibly know who she was. Nobody here in Poltoon knew who she was.

They chatted for a moment or two longer and by the time her mug of tea was empty, they had exchanged mobile numbers and agreed to meet the next time they were both free.

She watched as he strode away, his long legs covering the ground at a good pace. He was certainly great to look at and seemed to have a most attractive personality and a sense of humour with it. He was probably well aware of his charm and looks but then, wasn't she always conscious of her own appearance? She would have to watch her reactions to her pseudonym. Gina Hind. The initials were the same as her real name, Georgina Hetherington, and she now wondered if this could be a dead giveaway. Everyone had heard of the Hetherington Hotel chain. Whenever anyone asked her name, they always made the connection. There was even one of the hotels quite near here but right now, she had something to prove on her own terms. She looked round and saw Audrey frantically waving to her. She quickly went back inside, apologising to her boss as she collected the next tray of cups from an empty table.

*   *   *

Back in her rented flat, she reflected on what had become the highlight of her day. Jay Jacobs was everything that dear old Guy wasn't. She'd known Guy Westland all her life and her parents had desperately wanted them to marry. His family owned Westland

5

Hotels, another chain further north. It would be the dynastic marriage of the century for the hospitality world, a linking of two major players in the business. Fond of Guy though she was, marrying him was never a part of her plan. Her father had completely lost it when she told him she had refused Guy's marriage proposal.

'What's the matter with you?' he blustered. 'Can't you see he would be the perfect match for you? We've known the family for years. Most of your life. It's what we've always hoped for.'

'Well it isn't what I want. I'm not ready to be married. Especially not to Guy.'

'For heaven's sakes Georgina.' She knew he was angry whenever he called her by her full name. 'Pull yourself together. Life isn't some sunny dream of hearts and roses. You need to come down to earth and realise the truth. Guy's a good man. Everything you could possibly want.'

'Except I don't love him.'

That was four long weeks ago.

She sighed as she made herself an omelette, staring into space as the eggs congealed in the pan and turned into an inedible, rubbery mess. She tipped it into the bin and settled for a sandwich. Why was life so difficult? Much as she loved her parents, she was sick of them always trying to run her life. They gave her everything she wanted except the freedom to try new things. She had been working in one of their hotels for a while, as part of the management team. But whatever she did, it was controlled by the rules imposed by her father. So, just over a month ago, after a particularly angry exchange, she had rushed to pack.

'Where are you going darling?' her mother had asked, hovering near Georgie's bedroom door and looking a little teary.

'I have to get away Mummy. I'm feeling stifled. You both seem set on me marrying Guy and I don't love him. Not in the marrying kind of way. He's more like a brother to me. You can't organise every part of my life. I need some space. I'm going to see Jenny. Talking to her usually helps me sort out my brain.'

'But how long will you be away?'

'Don't know,' she snapped. 'I'll ring. Please, just give me some space.'

At this point her father had arrived on the scene.

'Don't be so ridiculous Georgina,' he said on hearing her rather sketchy plans. 'You're behaving like a spoilt brat. What's supposed to happen to the work you were doing at the Hetherington? Do I appoint someone else?'

'Your decision. I hardly make much of an impact on the place, do I? You've got so many rules about what has to be done and exactly how you want it achieved, a tame monkey could do the job if you showed it the right buttons to press,' she retorted. 'I need to do something on my own to prove I can. I'll be in touch when I'm ready.'

She had driven away in her expensive sports car, not caring where she was going. She always drove fast, but this time she was taking stupid risks. When she skidded round a corner, almost hitting a wall, she finally slowed down. Her heart was pumping with the adrenaline.

She parked outside her friend's flat and rang the bell. There was no reply and a neighbour leaned through her window and told her Jenny was away for a couple of weeks.

How could she have forgotten that? Where should she go now? Going back home was not an option. Not after she had finally found the courage to stand up to her father. She picked up the map book and at let in fall open at random.

She jabbed her finger onto the page and saw West Cornwall. 'Right,' she muttered under her breath. 'Cornwall it is then.'

*   *   *

After a couple of nights spent in a bed and breakfast, she decided to rent one of the many holiday apartments in the village of Poltoon.

Finding a temporary job had been relatively easy. The little café paid minimum wages and certainly didn't cover the rent of her apartment. For the time being, she was supplementing it with her credit card. Her father was right in one thing. She couldn't afford to live decently without his support. But, for now, she was at least managing some sort of independence.

Georgie sat looking over the beach as she ate her sandwich. It was a lovely apartment, small but perfect for her. As the height of the season approached, it would be more expensive to stay there. If she did stay in Cornwall for longer, she would have to find somewhere cheaper or get a better paid job.

As the beach was clearing of the families with small children, a different collection of people was taking over. Groups of teenagers were arriving, gathering together and often making fires. Slightly older people were filling the sea with surf boards, waiting for endless minutes for the one perfect wave. She hadn't ever tried surfing but it looked fun, as long as you were a very patient soul. She might give it a go herself one day. Meantime, it was much too nice an evening to be sitting inside. She picked up her bag and took a walk along the road. She climbed the cliff path and stood overlooking the little village. It was a good place to be. Life seemed to move at a much slower pace here and despite her aching feet, she felt totally relaxed and at peace.

She had scarcely given a thought to her future or how she was ever going to make the move back home. She watched the gulls wheeling around and screaming at each other. Amidst the noise, she realised her phone was ringing. She looked at the incoming call. Her mother. She hesitated before answering it but knew it would only cause extra hassle if she didn't take it.

'Hello Mummy,' she replied.

'Darling, where are you? Are you all right? When are you coming home? Your father and I are so worried about you.'

'You needn't worry. I'm absolutely fine. I've got a job and I'm working hard.'

'But where are you living? How are you managing?'

'Please Mummy. Stop asking so many questions. I have a rented apartment. It's really lovely. Overlooking the sea and it's very clean and yes, I am eating properly. I need time to sort out my life and decide on my future.'

'But where exactly are you? I can hear some sort of birds making a racket.'

'I told you before. I'm in Cornwall, in a little village. Please just settle for that. I don't want Daddy rushing down and dragging me back. I'll come back when the time is right. I promise. Okay?'

'But what are you doing? How are you managing to live?'

'Like I said, I'm working. Not getting very well paid but it's okay. I still have my credit card. I assume it's still all right for me to use it?'

'I suppose so, but I'm not sure your father will continue to support you if you persist in being so difficult. What exactly are you doing work-wise?'

'I love you Mummy. Please don't worry. Bye.' On that rather unsatisfactory note, she switched off her phone. Her mother was certain to call back and she didn't want to face further interrogation. There was no way she would admit to how little pay she was receiving. Undoubtedly, snobs that they were, they'd be horrified to think of their daughter serving teas and washing up in a beach café. If the worst came to the worst, she could always consider selling her beloved car.

She sat on her rock for a while longer, thinking. Was she really being terribly ungrateful for everything her parents had done for her? Probably, but she knew that inside she had something to prove to herself, if to no one else. It was difficult to explain to her parents, even to voice it to herself.

Suddenly she shivered. Dusk had fallen, almost without her noticing. She walked down the steep path again and looked up at the Clarence Hotel on the opposite side of the cliff. It was brightly lit and she could see people moving around behind the windows. Perhaps Jay was there. Perhaps he was, even now, looking out over the bay and seeing the same view that she was.

She looked forward to getting to know him. She hadn't even discovered what he did during their brief conversation. Was he a chef? A waiter? On the management team?

Why on earth was she so interested, when she knew virtually nothing about him? He was a good looking guy who happened to pass her way, and flatter her just a little. She should be used to flattery. Even without her usual hairdresser painstakingly looking after it each week, she was still proud of her long hair, despite the ridiculous cap she was forced to wear at work. Even so, Jay had been passing the café to look at her, according to what he had said, and he had no idea who she really was. He was seeing her for herself and not as some rich girl. She would try to get to know him better. Something had to relieve her lack of social life.

The surfing crowd were gathering at the top of the slipway, chatting and laughing. Most of them seemed older than she thought and she hesitated as she was passing them.

'Hello gorgeous,' one of them called to her. 'You want to come for a drink?'

'No thanks,' she muttered slightly nervously. She was out of her comfort zone and wasn't used to dealing with this sort of casual chat up. She had been wrapped in cotton wool for much too long. This was breakout time. Another day, she might just get the confidence to accept an invitation like this.

If she saw Jay again soon, she would certainly at least go for a drink with him. *Stalker?* She remembered her thoughts of earlier. Why on earth would anyone follow her for any reason more than he liked her? Nobody knew anything about her, so surely there could be nothing sinister in his approach?

CHAPTER TWO

Georgie went to work the next morning, hoping she might see Jay sitting on the sea wall at some point. She kept looking out during the morning coffee rush but he never arrived. She felt disappointed. Audrey asked if she was feeling all right, as she seemed so distracted.

'Sorry,' she replied. 'I was wondering if a friend might come in. I think he's put off by too many ladies drinking coffee.'

'It's funny that the men don't come inside. Do you think it's too feminine in here?'

'Maybe a bit floral for them. But, we do well enough with the female clientele, don't we?'

'Well, yes. I don't want to find myself in competition with the coffee chains because I simply couldn't keep up with them. I heard one of them is trying to get planning permission to move into this village. It will be the end of me if they do.'

'That would be a real shame. You really do provide a service for the people who like to be looked after as individuals, not one of dozens who drift through. Most of these ladies are regulars, aren't they? I don't see Mrs Ellis and her friend being an avid drinker of StarCosts or anything like them.'

'Doubt they could afford their prices anyway. I'll keep going as long as I can. Now, I'd better start getting the lunch things organised. You take a few minutes if you like, Gina. The tables are more or less empty now. We'll be run off our feet in an hour or so, though.'

She poured a coffee and went outside. She looked up the hill towards the Clarence. It was a medium-sized place, nothing like the size of any of their hotels. It may have a two or three star rating but she hadn't ventured close enough to check it out. She smiled to herself. She must have inherited some of her father's genes after all, if she was actually showing what could be termed a professional interest.

'So, another break is it, Gina?' a friendly voice said from behind her.

'Oh, Jay. I was wondering if you'd actually risk coming for a coffee this morning.'

'I've been busy and I suspect I've missed the witching hour.'

'We're just in the lull before the lunchtime trade. So, did you have a busy evening?'

'Very. We had a large party of people in for

a birthday meal last night. They hung around for what seemed like hours and there was still stuff to clear this morning.'

'What do you do?'

'Same as you. I'm a waiter. Just a temporary job of course.' He gave a nervous smile as he said it. 'I'm trying to earn a bit during the summer. One day, I shall have my own hotel and make my fortune.'

'Not a bad ambition. Dodgy though, especially in these times of austerity.'

'It will be many years before I can make it to those dizzy heights but I intend to be very good at what I do.'

'I'm sure you will,' Georgie replied, thinking he would charm his way into anything with his looks and easy grace.

'So, what's someone like you doing in a place like this?' he asked her.

'Like you. Holiday job, and sort of work experience.'

'Don't tell me you're also in this business?'

'Nothing formal. I'm still deciding on my future.'

'It's probably some time before you need to decide, isn't it?'

'Why do you say that?'

'Well, you can't be much over nineteen, can you?'

'I certainly can. I'm twenty-three, actually. I knew this wretched cap was a bad idea.'

'You don't look it. I'm a bit older. An

ancient twenty-five. Took me a while to decide where I wanted to go in life. Oh dear, I suspect the slightly red-faced lady behind the counter is trying to attract your attention.'

'Heavens. I've been sifting here for much too long. Sorry.'

'Let's meet tomorrow evening. I'm doing a day shift then so we can collapse together over a drink or something. I'll arrange for a bowl of warm water for each of us to be placed under the table, to soak our aching feet.'

Georgie giggled. It presented an amusing picture in her mind. 'Okay. Send me a text, where and when.'

'Will do.' He turned and went up the hill towards his hotel, grinning at her over his shoulder.

She liked this man. Really liked him. Her parents would undoubtedly consider him totally unsuitable for her, just as they'd done with everyone she'd ever brought home, other than Guy. They would dismiss him as a gold digger, bounty hunter or worse. At least she felt confident that he was chatting to her for her own sake and not in the hope of a step up in his career.

As she cleared tables, served food, took orders, washed up and generally helped Audrey, she thought about an evening out with Jay. It would be good to get to know him. She needed to work on her own cover story. Making some of it based on truth was always a good thing. She'd used the 'deciding what to do with her future' angle with Audrey and one or two other people she had met.

During the next afternoon, Jay sent her two texts.

Too many people here for me to take a break. How can they keep eating so much? x

A little later, a second one arrived.

I won't finish till 9 tonight. How about a coffee?

She replied:

I'd prefer a glass of wine. Beach Bar soon after 9? See you there, G.

Georgie grinned. As she cleared the little kitchen after they had closed, she found herself speculating once more about the date. It seemed almost strange not to have to tell anyone she was going out. No explanations were needed. No awkward introductions. Wasn't this exactly why she had run away from home in the first place?

'Run away' sounded far too dramatic for someone of her age but it did feel a little like that. Somehow, it proved that she wasn't being allowed to grow up by her parents. It felt good to be doing her own thing, meeting new people that hadn't been chosen or at least vetted by her parents.

'Gina, you can go now, love,' Audrey told her, breaking into her reverie.

'Oh, sorry, Audrey. I was miles away there,' she admitted.

'I thought you were. You've rubbed a hole in that cloth and the cooker's absolutely spotless. Thanks Gina. Have a nice evening. You doing anything special?'

'I'm meeting a friend later.'

'Not that gorgeous man you were chatting to earlier?'

'Well, yes, it is actually.'

'Lucky you. Just be careful though. You know what his type are like. Looking over your shoulder for the next one while they are kissing you.'

Georgie stared. 'Really? Why do you say that?'

'Oh, don't take any notice of me. I'm just an old fogey. Jealous that you're so young with all your life before you.'

'Don't say that. You're young at heart and you really enjoy running this place, don't you?'

'Course I do. Just end of the day weariness, I guess. You have yourself a good time.'

Georgie went back to her apartment and had a shower before deciding what to wear. There wasn't much choice. She took out a silk shirt, a favourite turquoise colour that looked okay over jeans, even if her mother would disagree that jeans were ever suitable for anything.

She was pleased with her choice. She wanted to prove to Jay that she was just an ordinary girl without revealing anything more than she wanted him to know.

It didn't occur to her that she was living any sort of lie. It was fun, taking on a new identity and creating her own past. She wondered where he lived. Was he inventing some sort of past as well? Did he have things to hide? She laughed to herself. This was just a casual acquaintance she was meeting for a glass of wine. Nobody special and never intended as anything more than a holiday fling.

She looked in the tiny fridge. She must do some shopping soon. She ate sandwiches or pieces of quiche at work but her diet was rather erratic at present. She needed to buy some fruit and salad and do something to improve matters.

She glanced quickly at her watch. It was just after seven o'clock now but she would easily have time to drive into the next town and visit the supermarket before meeting Jay at the bar.

*   *   *

It was busy, filled with holidaymakers buying suppers and dragging tired children round clinging to trolleys. Consequently, it was eight-thirty by the time she was loading her car and she felt hot and tired all over again. Too bad, she only had time to get the shopping home and unpacked. No time for any supper. Her better diet would have to start the next day.

At nine o'clock, she walked down to the beach and went into the bar. It was crowded and she looked around to see if she could see Jay. She was obviously there first. She bought a bottle of Pinot Grigio and took it and two glasses outside the bar.

There was a table at the edge of the terrace so she plonked the wine and glasses down, hoping to see Jay when he arrived. Quarter past came and went. Half past and still no sign of him. She poured a second glass and cursed herself for believing he ever really wanted to see her.

One of the surfers passed her and asked if the seat was free. She was tempted to say yes before she consumed the whole bottle of wine on her own, but she shook her head. Then she saw him. Her heart gave an extra beat as she waved to attract his attention.

'I'm so sorry,' he began. 'Thank you for waiting. I was scared you'd give up on me. We had a rush right at the end of my shift and I couldn't leave. What can I get you?'

'Nothing. Just sit down and help me with this before I finish the lot myself.'

'I'm starving. Do you mind if I order some chips or something?' he asked.

'Not at all. Sounds like a good idea.'

'Shall I get some for you too?'

'Please. I sort of missed supper.'

'Won't be long.'

She poured his wine and sipped her own. It was a warm evening and the sky was turning a pale azure blue over the sea. The sun left a few coppery streaks in the few clouds that hung around. The buzz of conversation around their table was muted as everyone enjoyed the lovely evening. Jay came back, nodding to a couple of other people as he passed them.

'So, what have you been doing with yourself?' he asked.

'Exciting stuff like grocery shopping after work. I was a bit late finishing too. Seems like the holiday season is getting going in earnest.'

'It will get very busy soon once the schools break up. This weather has dragged a few folk down early. Oh, just listen to us! All this small talk—we sound like an old married couple. Tell me a bit about yourself, Gina. Where do you come from? What's your background?'

'Hertfordshire. I'm an only one. Making a break from home and parents. They like to control what I do a bit too much for my liking,' she confessed.

'You don't seem the type to be attached to apron strings. I love that colour on you, by the way. Brings out the blue in your eyes.' He reached over and took her hand. He ran his fingers over her ring finger. 'No signs of anything permanent then?' he remarked casually.

'Of course not. Though there is, or was, someone I was seeing—back home.'

'What happened?'

'I just don't feel ready to settle and he wanted to.'

'So he obviously wasn't the one?'

'No. Besides, I've got a life to live. I want to experience much more than I have already.'

'I know what you mean. I'm hoping to travel. See other countries. I'd like to work in some hotels overseas and learn about life in other places and cultures. The Far East—even Australia and New Zealand.'

'Sounds ambitious. Trouble is, working in hotels is pretty much the same wherever you go. Far East is maybe a little more subservient, if you know what I mean. Staff are much more anxious to please and have to fight harder to keep their rather poorly paid jobs.'

He was staring at her and she bit her lip. She had said too much and probably given herself away completely.

'Well now,' he said thoughtfully, 'there's a girl who knows more than she was letting on. I take it you've been there?'

'Well, actually . . .' She paused. How much should she divulge? The family had always taken long haul trips, usually visiting other hotels whose owners invited them for holidays. 'I have a friend who works in different places. She's always sending me post cards from somewhere exotic and she tells me all about it.'

'And doesn't that inspire you to try it for yourself?'

'Maybe. One day. I'm rather liking the peace of Cornwall at present. Even if I never want to see another cream tea.'

'You're right, Cornwall is a pretty magical place.'

They finished their bowls of chips and the wine. It was getting late and she had an early start.

'I should go,' she said. 'Sorry but I start work at eight-thirty and I need my beauty sleep.'

'If that's what makes you so gorgeous to look at, I suppose I'll have to let you go. But I want to get to know you. I want to learn all about you and what makes you tick. You will see me again, won't you?'

'I'd like that. You haven't told me anything about yourself and I've been jabbering away all evening.'

'I'll walk you back home, wherever that is.'

'It's okay. Only round the corner. I've rented an apartment in the block back there, just for the time being, but I'll probably have to move out soon when the higher charges kick in.'

'Wow. Those places are gorgeous. Your job must pay well if you can afford to live there.'

'That's the problem. It doesn't pay well. I'm living on . . . well, savings,' she fibbed. 'So, where are you?'

'Nothing as glamorous. I'm staying in a caravan at the back of the hotel. They provide several of them for the staff. They have the policy that if we live in the hotel rooms, there's less space to rent out to the public.'

'That's terrible. Staff should have decent accommodation in a big hotel like that.' Her father always took care of his staff and provided good rooms and plenty of facilities for them. 'So, do you get to use the pool and things?'

'You must be joking. No, there are no perks at all. I suppose those of us who get a caravan to ourselves consider we are fortunate. Rentals in Cornwall come at a price. As you must know. Where will you go when you leave the apartment?'

'Haven't decided. Audrey and her husband live in a little cottage so there's no way she could take me in, even if I wanted her to, which I don't. She'd try to mother me even more than my parents do so that's not an option. Right, here we are. Thanks for the chips.'

'Thank you for the wine. My turn next time, assuming there will be a next time?' He reached over and took her hand, pulling her closer. Very gently, he kissed her lips. Feeling her respond, he took her in his arms and kissed her again. She felt him relax into a sigh and knew just how he felt.

'I must go. Text me when you have an evening free. Night.'

'Goodnight Gina.' He gave her a wave as she turned to let herself into her apartment block. She waved back and blew him a kiss, and then she floated up the stairs.

24

Guy had kissed her often enough, but it had never made her feel like this. Was she allowing herself to be carried away? Was it just some sort of holiday romance? Could she trust him?

She looked out of the window and watched as he climbed up the hill on the opposite side of the bay. She checked herself. Who on earth was she even to consider she may not be able to trust him? She was a total liar herself. She was lying about her background and even the name she was using was false. How could she be so two faced? Perhaps she should forget about trying to be someone else and confess all. The trouble was, as ever, she would never know if he liked her for herself or was it the fact that she came from a wealthy family. This was the precise reason for doing what she was.

No, she decided, she would have to continue with her assumed role for the time being.

Goodness, she had spent one evening with this man and she was already thinking of him as if he was someone special, almost as if he were the man she was about to marry. How naive was that? She had to allow herself to enjoy meeting him and stop trying to over analyse every little encounter. Her parents were probably right about her. She had far too little experience to be able to make any rational decisions. She made a vow to stop thinking about him.

*   *   *

Georgie neither saw nor heard anything from Jay over the next two days but she broke her vow at least twenty times each day. She tried to convince herself that he was just busy but there was always a nagging doubt that he actually didn't wanted to see her again. She debated endlessly with herself whether to send him a text or if that might look too pushy. In many ways, it was a totally new experience for her. Usually any men she met, even casual ones, were soon calling her to ask for a date. Her father was always convinced it was because of her background . . . something she found intensely belittling.

She was very attracted to Jay Jacobs, but she lacked confidence as never before. Clearly this was a time of soul searching, not to mention a way of finding out more about who Georgina Hetherington really was. A sobering thought.

Her phone rang and she grabbed it quickly, her heart racing. It was her friend Jenny. Usually she was delighted to speak to her but had to admit this time, her call was a disappointment.

'Hi Jenny. How are you?'

'I'm fine but what about you? I've had your mother pestering the life out of me to find out what I know about you and where you are. I said I hadn't spoken to you in ages. Exactly what is going on?'

'Oh Jenny, I can't begin to tell you. We had

a terrible row. Guy asked me to marry him and I turned him down. My parents freaked out when I told them and I had to escape for a while to save my sanity.'

'Poor old Guy. But if you don't want to marry him, there's no use pretending you do for their sakes. So what are you doing?'

'Working.'

'In one of the hotels?'

'Not exactly. Don't ask and then you won't have to lie if my parents ask you.'

'Well I hope you know what you're doing, Georgie.'

'I'm having fun. I've rented a flat. Only temporarily. I won't be able to afford it once the season starts. And I've met a gorgeous bloke. Early days of course but he is well . . . think a younger Antonio Banderas but with greenish rather than brownish eyes.'

'Be careful, Georgie. You're a hot property, my girl.'

'I'm . . . well, I'm in disguise. Sort of. Working under a pseudonym. I wasn't about to advertise whose family I belong to. I doubt I'd even have got this job if my boss knew. I think I'm safe. Jay likes me for just being me. Makes a change.'

'Jay? Oh, your Antonio character. He sounds gorgeous but please, take care. How did you meet?'

'He was hanging round the café. We just got talking. It's very early days so don't worry. I know what I'm doing.'

'I hope you do. Where are you exactly?'

'I think it's better if I don't tell you. I don't want my parents hassling you. I've told them I'm in Cornwall, so settle for that. Tell me about your holiday.'

'Mmm . . . my holiday with my new man of the moment. More of a Brad Pitt type but then, I always did go for the blonds.'

'I'd settle for Brad Pitt but so would most of the females in the world, and he's taken. So, where did you go?'

'Spain. We were staying in a lovely little mountain village. Peaceful and very warm.'

'And is this man "the one"?'

'Possibly. I'll let you know. Look, I've got to go now. Please take care of yourself, Georgie.'

'You sound like my mother. I know what I'm doing. Speak again soon.'

'Okay. Look after yourself. Bye love.'

She switched off her phone and stared at it, willing it to ring again. It did not oblige. Finally, Georgie plucked up her courage and sent a text.

Still busy? G x

There was no message in return. She went for a walk, taking care that she was always in range of a signal, which actually proved pointless. When she got back to her apartment, she cursed herself roundly for behaving like a lovesick teenager with no sense at all.

She made some hot chocolate and switched on the television, trying anything she could to distract herself. The truth was, she was lonely. She was seizing on someone's modest attention and making it into something much more. At least she always knew where she was with Guy, even if it was somewhere she didn't really want to be. But try as she might, she couldn't forget Jay's kiss; she wanted to feel that wonderful soaring sensation again.

*   *   *

She woke with a headache the next morning, and really wished she could take the day off work, but poor Audrey would be busy and would never find anyone else to cover for her. The young girl who came in to help on Saturdays would be at school today. Georgie could not let her employer down. As she stood under the shower, she felt pleased with her decision and sent a telepathic message to her father saying that he was wrong about her. She did have a sense of responsibility.

She set off for work, not even stopping for breakfast. Audrey always offered her toast and coffee, so she knew she could dawdle along and look at the beach, pristine after the tide had washed it overnight. She glanced at her phone and saw there was a message waiting. She hadn't even realised it was there.

Life is frantic. Far too busy for anything.

Can't afford to miss the overtime. I miss you, Gina. Can't wait to see you, soon I hope, xx

Her headache magically disappeared and she felt her heart lift again. It wasn't anything she had done to upset him and he still wanted to see her. Perhaps the only solution was to go for a meal at the Clarence Hotel. She could barely imagine the look of horror she might get from Jay if she did, though.

CHAPTER THREE

'Good morning Audrey,' she said brightly, pushing open the door of the little teashop. 'Isn't it a lovely day?'

'You sound cheerful. I expect you've seen your boyfriend again, have you?' Audrey asked.

'No, but he's very busy at work. He's on duty in the evenings at the moment so there's no time we're both free together.'

'Have you had breakfast?

'Not exactly.'

'Then you'd better make yourself some toast and coffee. I've got the scones baking already and the tables are done. You're early today.'

'Thanks. That would be great.' She made her breakfast and took it outside in the early sunshine. This place really was a small haven of calm at this time of day before anyone was about. The occasional dog walker was on the beach but no families had arrived yet.

'Now isn't that just the most lovely sight?' a voice said from behind her. Her heart seemed to turn over and she swung round.

'Jay. What are you doing here so early? I'd have thought you'd be sound asleep after all your late nights.'

'Too nice a morning to sleep in. I was just thinking how much I needed to see you and so here I am. Can I get some breakfast or aren't you open yet?'

'I can get you toast and coffee if you want.'

'That would be brilliant.'

'Give me five minutes. Or you can come inside if you like.' She barely rose from her seat before Audrey came to the door, a tray in her hands with more toast and a jug of coffee.

'I thought you might like something to eat,' she said to Jay.

'Gina was just telling me how little you were managing to see each other.'

'Well now, aren't you just the most thoughtful of ladies?' Jay said with a twinkle in his eye. 'Thank you. I'll settle up later.'

'On the house,' she replied, a blush staining her cheeks.

'Thank you, Audrey.' Georgie said. 'We won't be long.'

'Don't worry. I'll call you when I need you. Enjoy the morning while you can.'

'What a lovely lady,' Jay remarked.

'She's a sweetie. I feel very lucky to be working for her. So, tell me what's going on with you? I haven't seen you lurking around here at all these last few days.'

'I never lurk. Only stare at the prettiest girl in town. I've been pulling in extra shifts. I can't afford to refuse them, even if it means I miss seeing you.'

'I was thinking I might have to come for a meal one evening, if only to see you.'

'I shouldn't. Prices are at the high end of the market. Okay if you want to impress someone, but I wouldn't pay it.'

Georgie was interested. Her background always made her want to know what competitors were doing and charging for their products but she knew she would give herself away if she pried too much.

'Tell me about yourself, Jay. Where do you come from?'

'My family originate from Jersey but I've never lived there. I've lived in several places in England but hardly been anywhere outside of the country. School trip to France once but I was too young to learn much from it. Never done anything much career-wise but had a range of jobs in shops and then in the hospitality business. Like I said, I'm just working here for the summer. Reckon I'm learning a lot. People are strange creatures. The really wealthy clients are usually very polite and nice and the ones who've made loads of money recently are very demanding and often quite rude.'

'I know what you mean. The nouveau riche syndrome, we often call it.' He stared at her, puzzled at her knowledge. She blushed, knowing she was saying too much for the role she was playing. 'Do you want some more coffee?' she asked trying to change the subject.

'Thanks. It's good coffee. Probably better than the stuff we serve and charge a fortune for.'

'I'm addicted to it.' She laughed. 'So, do you think we'll ever get a day off together, Jay?'

'I'm off on Monday. All day and including the evening. We could do something if you like. What time do you finish?'

'Usually about half past five but I might get away earlier if it's quiet. That would be great. We could drive somewhere and have a meal?' She paused. Maybe he didn't have a car and her expensive sports model was a dead giveaway.

'I'd like that but I don't have a car.'

'I do. If you don't mind being driven by a woman.'

'Or we could have a picnic somewhere on the cliffs. We could have a walk and find a quiet spot.'

'That sounds lovely,' she replied. 'We can take wine and something delicious to eat. I'll get some bits and pieces.'

'Okay, deal. I'll buy the wine. Not much

good with food, I'm afraid. Left to me, it would be a pasty.'

'Much as I love pasties, we can do a bit better than that.'

It was almost nine o'clock and people were already drifting towards the beach. 'I suppose I should begin to earn my keep,' she said, getting to her feet reluctantly. He caught her hand for a heart stopping moment.

'I'll call you if I have a spare few minutes over the next few days. We might manage to see each other for a short time. I'm so sorry I can't offer you more.' He looked positively mournful and Georgie felt her heart reach out to him. If she went home to her family she could get him a much better job anywhere in their hotel chain.

'Anything you can manage. At least my hours are regular.'

'I could very easily fall in love with you but I have the feeling you may be out of my class.'

'Don't be silly. I'm a waitress in a beach café.'

'There's something about you. You have class. Your accent for a start and I feel there's a very different way of life behind you.' Georgie blushed. He was certainly quite astute.

'Quite the psychologist, aren't you?'

'I'm right though, aren't I, Gina? You learn a lot by looking at people.'

'This is all a bit deep for this time in the

34

morning.' She laughed. His perspicacity had thrown her a little. 'I need to start work now. Keep in touch and I shall look forward to our picnic on Monday. I'll text nearer the time if I can get away early.'

'Okay. Thank you and please thank Audrey for breakfast. Very kind of her. Bye, love.' He leaned over and kissed her on the lips. Though the kiss lacked the intensity of his previous one, it still managed to send Georgie's heart racing and made her feel quite light-headed.

'Bye Jay. Thank you for coming to find me.'

'My pleasure entirely. I'll be here the next time I can get away from serving breakfasts to the masses. These split shifts are killers. Bye, now.' He loped off, taking the hill in easy strides.

Georgie collected the dishes and mugs and stacked them on the tray. She felt strangely dreamy, as if she had woken from a deep sleep. Her feet seemed to be somewhere out of control. It was all quite ridiculous to feel like this because some handsome young man had complimented her. So what if her cover got blown? Did it matter as long as Jay really did have genuine feelings for her? She went inside and smiled at Audrey.

'Jay said to thank you very much. It was really kind of you.'

'Pleased to help young love on its way,' Audrey told her. 'He's certainly a handsome young man. If I was a few years younger, I might put up a bit of a challenge myself.'

'Go on with you. A happily married woman like you?'

'Doesn't stop you enjoying looking, whatever the age. Now, I suspect those two ladies will be coming in here any minute so let's get ready.'

*   *   *

Georgie's day was lightened by the stream of texts that came in every hour or so. She laughed at some of Jay's silly comments and felt closer to him than ever. Carrying trays, washing up and serving the many holidaymakers was fine. She completely forgot she had started the day with a headache and the time flew by.

Wasn't this why she had made her break from home for a while? She needed to know who she really was. All the same, Jay was clearly suspicious about her background. Should she wait a little longer before telling him the truth? She was almost certain that he didn't know who she was but she hated the lies. It was not yet time to change things. Poor little rich girl. Always afraid that someone would like her only because she was rich. If she ever had children of her own, she would make certain they didn't grow up feeling the way she did. No wonder her parents favoured Guy so much. He had his own fortune to inherit so there was no way he was after her money.

The weekend seemed to crawl by but at last Monday arrived. She had told Audrey about their proposed picnic and she provided some slices of fresh quiche and made up a dish of salad towards it.

'You can leave once the teas are over. I'll manage after five o'clock,' Audrey said.

'You're very kind. I'd like to pop to the delicatessen too. A few olives and so on.' She was determined that everything would be special for the evening. Perhaps his romantic idea of a picnic was to cover the fact that he didn't want to spend money on a meal out. With the hours he was working, he surely couldn't be too badly off? She gave a shrug. Whatever the problem, nothing was going to spoil the evening ahead.

She sent him a text to say she would be ready by five-thirty. That would give her time to go home, shower and change. She felt ridiculously excited as if this was some sort of turning point in her life. But it was simply the first time she had found someone herself, without her parents introducing them. For a moment, she imagined Jay in formal evening dress, mingling with the sort of people that moved in her home circle.

*   *   *

Georgie packed the picnic things. She left her

hair hanging loose and wore a favourite skirt and matching top. It wasn't windy for once so she could enjoy a change from the eternal jeans she seemed to live in. She added a cotton jacket, knowing it might get chilly later.

She looked out of the window and saw Jay walking into the car park below the flats. She grabbed her bag and keys, locked the door and ran down the stairs to meet him. He was carrying a large back pack and he reached out for the picnic bag. 'Goodness, it feels as if you've packed enough to feed the five thousand. You look nice. Very summery.'

He was wearing light coloured trousers and a smart summer shirt in an olive green that seemed to match his eyes. They were definitely green, she decided.

'You look pretty good yourself. So have you decided where we're going?'

'I thought we might climb behind the hotel and walk along the top. There's a nice little cove on the other side if we feel suitably energetic.'

'Sounds great. I haven't been that way.'

They were both panting slightly by the time they reached the top. It was a warm evening and the steep path took them high above the village.

'Looks different from this side,' Georgie commented. 'You can see much further along the coast. What's that town I can see in the distance?'

38

'St Ives, if that's the one you mean.'

'I thought that was much further away.'

'It is quite a long way. It's a clear evening so the light's good. Means you can see far into the distance. The height of the cliffs makes a difference too. You good to move on? It's level for a while before the drop down again.'

'I'm fine. We weren't too busy today.'

'Sorry. We can stop here if you're tired.'

'No, course not.'

'Give me your hand. I can always pull you along.'

'As well as carrying the food and drink? What a man!' She gave him her hand and immediately felt the thrill of contact. She gave him a squeeze and he looked at her and grinned.

'I can't believe we actually have a whole evening together at last. These snatched moments just aren't enough, are they?'

'I guess not. Now you have the chance to tell me all about yourself. Your turn to talk, Jay.'

'Not much to know really. I have a brother and sister, both older than me and living near the Devon border. Two parents, still together despite several hiccups over the years. Went to a large comprehensive sort of school and got decent exam results. Messed around for a while and worked in all sorts of places until I decided on the hospitality route. That's about it for a potted history of me. But what about you? You've said very little about yourself. I

39

really know nothing about you.'

Georgie found herself blushing a fiery red. Where on earth did she start? Telling him slight truths would be too obvious. She needed to invent a whole background if she wanted to maintain her cover.

'I live in Hertfordshire. Well, my parents do. I went to a sort of grammar school, I suppose.' She laughed nervously. Her very expensive private school was possibly similar to a upmarket grammar school. 'Exams were okay but like you, I couldn't really decide what to do. I didn't want to go to university, though my parents wanted me to.'

'There was no question of me doing that. I had to work and earn my own money. My parents couldn't have supported me, in any case.'

'That's sad if you wanted to go. Couldn't you get a grant or something to help with the costs?'

He frowned slightly and looked away from her.

'I didn't contemplate it,' he said. 'I did everything from stacking shelves in the supermarket to working as a builder's labourer. Anything to earn money. Right, here we are. Can you manage this track? It's steep but well worth the effort. We can take a different route back so don't worry about having to climb back up again later.'

She knew she should have worn more

sensible shoes. The sandals were not really strong enough for this sort of activity so she slipped and slithered her way down, grabbing at stout heathers as she went.

'Sorry, I should have warned you what I had in mind,' Jay apologised. 'Stay there and I'll take the stuff down and come back to help you down the last bit.' He strode ahead, making light of the steep path with loose rocks designed to trip the unwary. He dumped the bags and came back, holding out two hands to steady her.

'Sorry, I'm being a wimp, Jay. Too fashion conscious to wear something sensible on my feet,' she said with a grin.

'I wouldn't change a thing. You are lovely in every way.'

When they reached the bottom, he pulled her close to him and she melted into his arms. He kissed her nose and laughed, wiping away the moisture from her forehead with his thumb. 'Sorry, that climb was a bit more than you bargained for.'

'Not at all. I enjoyed the way you helped me down the last bit.' He held her close again and she felt him sigh. He picked up the bags and led them down to the base of the cliffs where there was soft, dry sand. He unpacked his rucksack and produced a rug.

'I never thought of that. Shall I unpack the food?'

'Let's paddle first. I thought I'd chill the

wine at the edge of the sea. I couldn't manage to keep it cool in the bag, not without making the rug damp. I got Pinot Grigio again as I thought you liked that.'

'Lovely,' she said, slightly disappointed he hadn't brought champagne or something sparkling, at least. She cursed herself silently, knowing it was snobbish. Guy would never have brought anything less than champagne but then, he would never have suggested a romantic picnic on a beach in Cornwall.

Why was she even thinking of the man she had rejected? Looking at the gorgeous man before her, she knew that Guy came nowhere near him in any way.

'Come on. Take those sandals off and let's bathe those tired feet of yours.'

They ran over the sand, hand in hand like a pair of kids and were soon splashing in the waves.

'It's freezing,' she moaned. 'I hope you've got a towel in that bag of yours.'

'You'll have to dry off naturally. I can always rub them dry with my shirt . . .'

'I wouldn't dream of it. I dare say I'll survive. But now, I'm starving. Can we go and eat?'

'Of course. The wine seems to be chilled too. You're right. This water is freezing. Come on.' He grabbed her hand and almost dragged her back up the beach.

'It's gorgeous here. So isolated. Not a soul

in sight.'

'I hoped you'd like it. One of my favourite places. I've been coming here for ages. We had holidays in the area when we were kids so I've known it for years. Wow, Gina, you've done us proud here—this is a feast, not just a picnic!'

'Audrey gave us quite a bit of it. She's so kind.' She didn't want him to feel uncomfortable, thinking she had spent a lot of money on the delicacies, even if she had been a little extravagant at the deli.

The meal over, she lay back, looking up at the gulls wheeling around overhead. Jay moved the empty containers and rolled to her side. He pushed an arm behind her head and gently pulled her close.

'Gina,' he whispered. 'I've been waiting for this moment for a long time.' He kissed her until her mind was whirling and her senses were in turmoil.

CHAPTER FOUR

It was the most perfect evening. Anything Georgie had ever done in her varied past was forgotten, so swept away was she by this moment. She kissed Jay's eyes, his face, his lips. He rolled over to one elbow and looked down at her. His thumb was relentless in stroking her wrist, sending waves of . . . of

43

something new and unfamiliar, washing over her.

'You are so beautiful. I can't believe my luck in finding you. I don't want this evening to end. I love seeing your hair spread out behind you like a golden fan.' He bent to kiss her again and she felt her body seem to float into space in that wonderful, unique way that first time he had kissed her. She would have liked it to go on forever but a sudden shiver made her realise she was growing cold. 'We should move,' he whispered. 'You're shivering, Gina.'

'I don't want it to come to an end either but the light is going. I don't fancy walking along these cliffs in the dark.'

'We don't have to. If we follow the path inland a bit, there's a road that goes back to the village. We might even catch a bus going our way if we're really lucky.'

'I didn't realise a road came so close to this beach.'

'There's no car park anywhere so it remains secluded. People rarely walk far from their cars so it's only ever found by walkers and people who know it's here.'

They packed up everything, tucked it all into Jay's rucksack and set off, holding hands as if they couldn't bear to be parted. Conversation was less intense and they enjoyed the walk, chatting easily. The gulls were flying back to their cliff-top homes and jays wheeled over, clattering their raucous cries as they found their perches.

Hedgerows were filled with the scent of wild garlic. The white flowers made bright borders at the roadside, so even in the gathering darkness their route was marked. Stars were beginning to show until they were close to the lights from Poltoon, making it more difficult to star gaze.

'I know we need street lights but it stops you seeing the stars, doesn't it?' Georgie said.

'Oh, look! There's a shooting star.'

'You should make a wish,' Georgie told him. 'I missed it.' He closed his eyes briefly, then he smiled.

'Guess what I wished for?'

'No, don't tell me or it won't come true.'

'Okay. But I'm pretty sure it will. I feel it in my bones.' He slowed her down and once more, drew her close and kissed her. 'I'm becoming addicted to your kisses,' he remarked.

'Oh Jay, how long will it be before you get another day off?'

'I don't know. They post overtime once we get the rotas. There's competition for it but I get there first.'

'But surely you don't have to take every bit of overtime?'

'Pay's pretty poor so I'm afraid I do.'

Georgie sighed. This was going to prove a frustrating relationship if they could see each other so rarely.

'We'll have to take to midnight walks, I guess,' she said with a wicked grin.

'Won't do much for your early rising regime.'

'True. I'll just have to sleep in the evenings.'

'I love your openness and honesty,' Jay told her. She was glad it was dark and he couldn't see her blushes. Open? Her? If only he knew! 'So, is Gina short for Georgina?' he asked.

'Yes. I always knew when my parents were angry when they used my full name.'

'I can't imagine anyone ever being angry with you.'

'You don't know me that well. I can be quite stroppy when I'm annoyed,' she admitted.

'Then I'll have to make sure I don't annoy you.'

They reached the road leading to her apartment and paused. 'I need to give you the picnic containers.' He opened the bag and handed over the empty boxes.

'Thanks, Jay. You said there was enough to feed an army but I notice it all disappeared.'

'I know. I can't stop once I've started eating,' he grinned. 'It's been a perfect evening. I'll text you when I'm free again. Thank you so much for coming.'

'Thank you. I've had a lovely time. Nobody's ever taken me for a picnic like that before.'

'We'll do it again soon. I suppose it's a bit limiting walking everywhere, though.'

'I do have a car tucked in the garage. We

could go further afield next time. I'm happy to drive.'

'We'll see. I'll call you soon. Goodnight my lovely Gina.'

'Goodnight Jay. Sleep well and thank you again.'

She stood on tiptoe and reached up to kiss him just once more. He kissed her back then very gently pushed her away.

'If you do that again, I may not be able to part with you at all. We'd be entering dangerous territory. Night,' he said, turning away quickly. She watched until he went round the corner and was out of sight.

'Goodnight Jay. Perhaps next time I won't let you part with me,' she whispered to the night air.

She shivered and went inside. What exactly was she thinking? Did she want to make this sort of commitment on so short an acquaintance? She knew very little about him really, although she felt she didn't need to know any more. He was everything she could want in a partner, wasn't he? Intelligent, good looking, tall and slim. Everything that Guy wasn't. Or was she being too naive?

She washed up the plastic containers, deep in thought. Later in bed she lay wide awake, reliving the magical evening. How could something so simple take on such significance? She should convince herself that this was just a bit of fun, free of her parents' control and something to enjoy.

At last she fell asleep and woke late. A quick shower and she rushed off to work, knowing breakfast would have to rely once more on Audrey's generosity.

*   *   *

'So, how did it go last night?' Audrey demanded as she arrived in the kitchen.

'It was lovely. We walked along the cliffs and climbed down to a little cove for the picnic. Bit steep and I stupidly went in sandals. Gorgeous evening, though. We even paddled in the sea. Freezing cold.'

'Sounds lovely, dear. A nice simple evening in beautiful Cornwall. And when are you seeing him again?'

'Don't know, depends on his shifts and overtime.'

'He's certainly a hard worker, I'll give him that. I'm surprised they give him so much overtime.'

'So am I really. But he's taking a course somewhere and needs to save up to pay for it.'

'Such a shame you kids have to pay for education. He maybe doesn't want to take on a loan. Now, I expect you need some coffee and toast? Help yourself love.'

'I hope you don't mind me having breakfast like this every day?' Georgie asked.

'Course not. Least I can do. You're a good

worker and reliable. I think the profits can stand a slice or two of bread.'

'I could do with that in writing,' Georgie mumbled.

'What do you mean?'

'Nothing. Just someone I know who thinks I'm incapable of doing anything much. Can I make some toast for you?'

'No. You're all right.'

'I'll stay inside today. It's looking a bit damp out there.' She sat at one of the tables near the window and watched the few hardy people walking their dogs. It was drizzling a bit and a complete contrast to yesterday's golden evening.

Her heart gave a small leap as she saw a figure rushing down the hill. She was sure it was Jay and she stood up, anticipating that he would come into the café to share breakfast again. But he turned off and leapt onto the bus, as it was drawing away from the stop. Strange. He didn't mention going anywhere today and she was certain he'd said he was working.

She fingered her mobile phone in her pocket, wondering if she should text him. It might look as if she was chasing him. She ate her toast and wondered where he was going. Perhaps it wasn't him. There must be any number of tall dark men around and she could have been mistaken. But she knew she wasn't.

*   *   *

It was a busy day and though she looked out of the windows several times, she didn't see Jay again.

At the end of the day, she felt the evening looming large and empty. She decided that she must do something. She settled for the cinema as it was still damp and dreary. She hated the idea of going alone but there was no choice. At home or working in one of the hotels, it was easy. People were coming and going all the time and she was always being invited out.

It was quite a small cinema but it had three screens to choose from and surprisingly, the films were all recent releases.

As she was coming out, she saw the crowds coming from the other showings. In front of her was a tall dark man, his arm round the shoulders of a small, dark haired female. She seemed to be leaning close to him. Georgie paused, looking into a mirror on the wall to see if she could catch a reflection. She felt convinced it was Jay and she hurried after him, torn between wanting to see him and dreading that it was him.

By the time she'd got outside, the man and girl had disappeared. Why on earth should it be Jay? She was letting her imagination run away with her and seeing him in places he could not possibly be.

She went to her car and drove back to

50

Poltoon, cursing herself for being so stupid. All the same, she felt unsettled. After the magic of the previous evening, it didn't seem possible that Jay could be out with someone else. Besides, he had clearly said that he was working for the next few days.

She switched her phone on and there was a text waiting from Jay. It had been sent at eight o'clock, when she was watching the film so he couldn't possibly have been in the cinema.

Missing you today. Great evening yesterday. See you soon, my lovely Gina xx

Georgie grinned and sent a text back.

Hope so. Evenings are long on my own. Let me know when you are free again. Love G xx

*   *   *

It was two days before he contacted her to ask if she would meet him for a drink. They met at the beach bar, as before. This time, he wasn't late and he had bought a bottle of wine.

They sat close and chatted about their work and exchanged funny little anecdotes about things that had been happening. It was relaxed and comfortable, though Georgie kept trying to convince herself that she mustn't make too much of it. At the end of the evening, he walked her back to the apartment.

'Are you going to invite me in for a coffee?' he asked.

'Of course, if you'd like to. Only instant, I'm

afraid.'

'Instant is fine. I'm not even sure I need any coffee. Just the chance to be with you a while longer.'

They went up the stairs and she let him in. He looked out of the window while she went nervously into the kitchen. Was she being foolish? What was he expecting?

'Quite a view from here, isn't it?'

'I think so. Sadly, I've only got one more week to go and then I'll have to find somewhere else. Prices take a hike after that.'

'Shame. Everywhere gets expensive though. Have you had any thoughts about what you'll do?'

'Haven't a clue. Shall have to start looking though. There's bound to be somewhere. The kettle's boiled. I'll go and make the coffee.'

'Come here. Never mind the kettle.' He pulled her close and kissed her, feeling her body move closer to his. 'Oh, Gina, I want you so much.' She froze, realising exactly what he meant. She didn't know how to cope.

'You're a lovely man. But I . . . I'm not ready for anything more yet. Please, can we slow things down a little? We hardly know each other.'

'I'm sorry. I must have misread the messages you're giving me.' He let her go and drew away from her. 'Perhaps you really were only offering coffee.'

'I'm sorry Jay. I'm very fond of you. I even

52

think I might be just a little in love with you but . . . I think it might be rushing things a bit.'

'I thought you were . . . Your last text, well you signed with Love. I thought you meant just that.'

'I often sign with love. Look, I'm sorry. I'll make some coffee.' She spooned powder into two mugs, shaking slightly. She prayed that she hadn't ruined everything. She didn't want to lose him but if he really was after . . . well, just the one thing everyone talked about, she needed to be more sure of her own feelings first.

'Do you take sugar?'

'No, just black please. I'm sorry Gina. I didn't want to make you feel uncomfortable. But you are always so responsive when we kiss. I thought it was what you expected.'

'Maybe it is . . . maybe it is what I want but I need a little more time, that's all.'

'I take it you're not exactly experienced?' he asked gently. She blushed. It almost seemed like making an embarrassing childish confession. 'Sorry. You don't have to answer that. So tell me, what have you been doing with these long evenings?'

'I went to the cinema. Quite enjoyable but not so much fun on your own.'

'I agree. Perhaps we could go together one evening. There are a couple of good things coming soon.'

'Great. I'd like that. Do you go often?'

'Not that often. I've only seen a couple of things since I've been here.'

She prodded a little, to try and see if it really could have been him at the cinema the other evening but he said nothing to raise her suspicions. It was the right decision to postpone anything more with him, especially if she felt unsure of him. When he had finished the coffee, he got up and stretched his long limbs.

'I'd better get moving. Early breakfasts tomorrow. Then a break and the lunchtime shift. Another break and it's the evening shift. Quite a day.'

'Sounds dreadful. No time to really unwind and it seems to go on day after day. Exhausting.'

'I manage. I have a lot of stamina.'

'Jay, I'm sorry if I've disappointed you . . .' She reached out to touch his hand.

'Don't worry. I'm sorry I misinterpreted your messages.'

'I hope you'll still want us to see each other?'

'Of course. Gina, I'd hate you to think that was all I wanted from you. You're a very special person. I want to get to know everything about you. What makes you tick. What you like and what you hate. I want to please you in every way possible. Now, am I allowed another kiss or do you want me to leave you in peace?' She made no reply but drew him close to her in answer.

'I'm going now. I'll see you soon, if you want to.'

'Of course I do. Just give me a little more time to get used to the idea of something more.'

'Good night, Gina.'

He left her feeling totally confused. She knew she had done the right thing but it didn't stop her longing for him. She needed to speak to Jenny. Was eleven o'clock too late to phone? She dialled the number and reclined on the sofa. The imprint of Jay's head was still on the cushion and she nestled into it, almost sensing the scent of him still lingering. Jenny answered at last.

'Georgie? What's up?'

'I needed a chat. Have I interrupted anything?'

'No, I was just on my way to bed. Is everything all right?'

'Yes. No. Oh, I don't know Jenny,' she groaned.

'Is this the gorgeous hunk? What's gone wrong?'

'Nothing. He's wonderful. He wanted to move things on a stage and I said no. I'm afraid I may have blown it but he says he still wants to see me. Was I being stupid to say no?'

'Of course not. You'll know when it's right. If he dumps you, then he isn't the right one.'

'I'm getting neurotic. He says he likes my

openness and honesty but everything he knows is a lie. Should I confess all?'

'I wouldn't. Not until you know where it's leading. Come on Georgie, you're a grownup now.'

'My parents never allowed me to be grown up. That's the whole problem. Everything here is based on pretence.'

'So what have you been doing?'

'We went for a romantic beach picnic the other night. Quite magical. I've never done that with anyone before. I went to the cinema one evening.'

'Without the handsome escort?'

'Yes. He was working.' She paused, remembering the man she had seen who so reminded her of Jay.

'What is it?' Jenny asked. She was just too darned perceptive, Georgie thought.

'Oh, nothing. Just part of me seeing him round every corner when he couldn't possibly be there.'

'You've got it bad, haven't you love? Look, why don't I come down for a weekend and we can chat properly? I assume you can put me up?'

'The sofa makes into a bed so yes, as long as I'm still in this apartment. I've to move out next week, when the prices go up.'

'Surely you can afford it?'

'Well, as long as Daddy keeps paying for my credit card.'

'Of course he will.'

'I'm not so sure. He's pretty angry with me for rebelling. Hey, it would be great to see you. When can you come down?'

'I might make it this weekend.'

'I might have to work on Saturday. But I'll try to take some time off. There's a Saturday girl.'

'Deal. I'll drive down Friday afternoon and be with you for the evening. What's the address?'

Georgie gave it to her and they finished the call. It would be great to see Jenny with time to talk properly. She'd know the right thing to do.

CHAPTER FIVE

When Georgie told her boss of her plans, Audrey immediately offered to find cover so she could take Saturday off.

'That's so kind of you. Are you sure you can manage?'

'We're often relatively quiet on Saturdays as it's changeover day. People leaving and new visitors haven't arrived. I'm sure Maddy's friend will come in to help. She came in last year. You have a nice time with your friend. I've been worried that you don't have much of a life down here.'

'I must admit, I'll enjoy a good gossip with Jenny. I've known her for years.'

'Now, you get yourself some breakfast while you can.'

She took her toast and coffee to one of the outside tables and glanced up the hill towards the Clarence Hotel. She wished she would see the tall dark man coming down the hill to join her but undoubtedly, he was busy serving breakfasts.

She was still trying to convince herself she had made the right decision but she knew she had missed something she really wanted. She hoped she hadn't ruined everything. Just the thought of him excited her. Being even closer was positively thrilling. She was already halfway towards making her mind up. Given another chance, she might not say no. Jenny would be here soon and her more experienced friend would be certain to give her good advice.

She picked up her empty cup and plate and went back inside. It was a rather boring life in truth but she was determined to stick to the job for a while. She was proving something to herself and felt proud of it.

There were two texts from Jay during the day. She felt relieved that he was still interested in her. She told him about Jenny's planned visit, assuming he'd be working all weekend as usual at the hotel. Much to her surprise, he suggested they might meet up on the Sunday.

I'd love to meet your oldest friend, he texted. *What about coffee on Sunday morning?*

That sounds great. Come round to the apartment. G xx

*   *   *

Jenny arrived in time for supper and greeted Georgie with great affection.

'Gosh you're looking great. This place suits you. I love it. Lovely views and such a pretty village. So where's the action round here?'

'There's not exactly much action anywhere. The Beach Bar is okay but hardly a hub of activity. I've become very reclusive. I've even spent time watching television.'

'Good grief. You are Georgina Hetherington, aren't you? I haven't found someone posing as her?'

'Actually, I'm not Georgina Hetherington at all. I'm Gina Hind to everyone round here.'

'Heavens. I'll never remember that. Will it matter if I call you Georgie?'

She frowned, thinking of Jay meeting her friend.

'I'd rather my cover wasn't blown just yet. Gina is who Jay thinks I am. Did I mention he's coming for coffee on Sunday?'

'Only about four times. I take it I'm supposed to give you a star rating?'

'I guess that's the idea. He wants to meet

59

you but I suspect his plan is to discover more about me. I'm really not sure it's a good idea.'

'Oooh, I do. I need to inspect him and give you my report. From what you've said so far, I gather he's an alpha male in all physical respects but you're a bit hazy on the rest. Something he's holding back? But that may be on account of you hiding about ninety percent of yourself behind this Gina Hind character. Anyway, enough of this speculation. I can smell something cooking and I'm starving. What's for supper?'

'Nothing special. Just some lasagne from the café. Audrey, that's my boss, made an extra dish for us. She's brilliant actually. Really thoughtful.'

'She sounds nice. You can take me there for coffee tomorrow and I'll do a survey of the workplace too.'

They ate the meal and washed it down with a decent bottle of Italian wine. Georgie chatted non-stop, making up for the many quiet evenings she had been spending alone. Much of the conversation centred round Jay of course and a little on Jenny's new man.

'You seem quite keen on this chap,' Georgie remarked.

'He's lovely. It's all very relaxed and we have a lot in common. He's quite keen on riding so that's a good start. He's got a lovely chestnut gelding and I've taken Starlight over to his place to stable her. Works out more easily when we want to go out together.'

'All sounds pretty serious. And you've been away together?'

'Yes. We're thinking of getting married but not for a while as he has several large projects on the go. Once he's got the contracts completed, then we shall name the day.'

'Oh Jenny, that's wonderful. I'm so happy for you. I can't wait to meet him.'

'You'd have met him by now if you weren't stuck in this place. How long do you intend to stay here?'

'I don't know. I had to prove I could do a proper job and support myself. Not that I'm exactly doing that. Daddy's still paying for this place even if he doesn't realise it yet. I'm waiting for the credit card to be refused at any moment.'

'Tell me exactly what's been going on with your man. Romantic meals? Clubs? Long strolls by the sea?'

'Not really.' Georgie bit her lip. Thinking about it, they'd spent very little time together at all. 'He's working crazy hours to save up for his hospitality course. Doesn't get much time off and I think he gets a very poor rate of pay.'

'In other words, he doesn't spend anything on you.'

'Well, no. But is that important? Isn't this what it's all about? I don't need to be impressed with lavish entertaining or presents. It's quite a novelty for me. He's with me for my sake and not because he thinks he might gain something. If he knew my real background, I'd have to find him a better job and in any case, he'd probably be afraid of me because of it.'

'I hope you're right Georgie. With so short a friendship, I think you were absolutely right to hold back. I know we have a similar background but I've been out in the big wide world a lot more than you. My parents wanted me to be independent while yours were much more the wrap you in cotton wool types. You're quite an innocent where men are concerned.'

'I could almost hate you for being so right.'

'Come on love. I'm speaking the truth and I don't want you to be hurt. Maybe your Jay is the perfect man and it will all work out. All I'm saying is you don't know him very well yet and you shouldn't rush into anything you can't handle. You're enjoying freedom for the first time in your life and Jay's obviously everything dear old Guy isn't.'

'Guy has never roused the same feelings in me as Jay does. With Jay, just a touch seems to send me to jelly. We stretched out side by side on a blanket on the beach looking up at the stars. When did Guy even notice there were any stars?'

'Okay. I get the picture. But you'd never live without decent money behind you. You're too used to buying whatever you want, whenever you want it. You've been all over the world, staying in the best hotels. Enjoying good food and fine wines.'

'But Jenny, isn't this the point I'm making here? I haven't missed any of that. I'm just as happy with a beach picnic as an expensive meal in an over-priced restaurant.'

'Novelty, my girl. Believe me, you'd hate to live the rest of your life that way.'

'But we wouldn't have to. Once we were sure of each other, he could work for my father in one of the hotels. He's getting qualifications and he's clever, I know it.'

'Clearly you're besotted. Now, are we going to explore the Beach Bar or whatever delights this place has to offer?'

'If you like. Or we can stay here and open another bottle.'

'I need a bit of a walk. It seemed a long drive and sitting so long doesn't suit me. Come on. I'll pay if you're broke.'

*   *   *

The bar was packed with crowds of surfers and holidaymakers having their final evening out before returning home. It was noisy and lively and gave no chance for further conversation. Several people invited them to join them but Jenny grinned and shook her head. She bought a bottle of wine and they perched on a rail at the edge of the terrace outside.

'Bit mad in there,' Jenny shouted.

'No kidding. That's where Jay works,' she shouted back, pointing up the hill towards the hotel.

'We should go there for a meal tomorrow night.'

'No way.' Georgie laughed. 'He'd be furious. We'll go somewhere nice though.'

They finished the wine hurriedly and left the bar to get away from the noise. They walked along the road beside the beach and rested elbows on the wall, looking out at the waves as they rolled endlessly onto the shore. It was a gentle, peaceful scene. The service bus stopped outside the bar and Georgie looked back at the passengers getting off. There was a tall, dark man among them. He turned and walked briskly up the hill. She gave a gasp. It had to be Jay. Jenny looked at her friend and followed her gaze.

'That's him, isn't it?'

'I think so. But it can't be, Jenny. He said he was working this evening.'

'Maybe he wasn't. Perhaps something or someone called him away. Didn't he get off the bus?'

'I think so. Maybe it wasn't Jay at all. I only got a glimpse and there could be several tall, dark people working at the hotel—or staying there.' She was trying hard to convince herself that it wasn't Jay but she remembered the man she saw at the cinema the other night. She had also seen him catching the bus early one morning, when he'd said he was working.

'So, maybe Jay isn't quite perfect after all.'

'Maybe not. But then, I'm not who he thinks I am either. Perhaps we're a pair of con artists both out to cheat the other. Shall we go back?'

However cheerful she tried to be, the evening was spoiled for Georgie. Jenny sensed it and tried to comfort her.

'You know, there's no commitment between you. If he has a life he hasn't told you about, he's no worse than you.'

'I wanted there to be a commitment.'

'It will happen when it's right. No use trying to hurry it. He's clearly holding something back. He's not spending money even if he's earning it. What has he done for you? Bought a few bottles of wine and a picnic for goodness sake.'

'I provided the food,' she said in a small voice. 'For the picnic, I mean . . .'

'Then he should be rolling in dosh. Whatever you say, waiters in posh hotels get decent tips if nothing else, and a good looking bloke will get more than most. I'll reserve my final judgement till I've met him but I'd say you'd be well out of it.'

'But I don't want to be out of it,' she replied miserably. 'Now I'm even more confused and you were supposed to make me feel good about it all. I like him so much.'

'Come on my girl. You need some coffee. Too much wine and too much soul searching.

Tomorrow, we're going out for the day. Do some shopping, visit places and maybe go to a club if we can find one somewhere.'

'Okay. If you say so. I could do with some more clothes. I came away with just a small travel bag and I've worn everything to death.'

*   *   *

The two girls began their day with breakfast at the café. Audrey was delighted to see them and touched that Georgie had brought her friend to meet her.

'On the house,' she insisted.

'What a great boss to have.' Jenny laughed. 'It's very kind of you but there's no need.'

'My pleasure. Now it's apricot jam you like best, isn't it?'

'You know me too well already.'

Georgie kept glancing up the hill throughout their meal, as if looking for clues about Jay's activities. Wisely, her friend made no comment.

'What are you planning to do today, Gina?' Audrey asked as she brought a fresh pot of coffee.

'Just looking around. Bit of shopping maybe.'

'Enjoy yourselves. She's a hard worker, this friend of yours. Deserves a day off. Here come the girls now. I'd better go and sort them out.'

'Hard worker, are you Gina?' Jenny said

with a laugh. 'I can't believe you call yourself Gina. Georgie isn't exactly giving anything away.'

'I know, but it seemed like a complete change for me. I was taking on a whole new identity. Surely the fact that Audrey thinks I'm a hard worker says something?'

'Okay. You win. Come on. Let's go and spend some money. Your car or mine?'

'I'll take mine. Give you a break from driving.'

Jenny could hardly believe Georgie was the same friend she'd always known. Gone was the frivolous girl who bought anything and everything that took her fancy. She spent money carefully and chose simple things with no discernible label.

'My goodness. You are being frugal.'

'I don't need a lot. Shorts, jeans and T-shirts seem to be the order of the day here. I've got a few things for being smart but I rarely seem to need much more.'

'How long is this going to go on for?' Jenny asked. 'You can't seriously want to live like this forever.'

'Of course not. I'll probably see out the season. Go back in a couple of months maybe. Audrey wouldn't keep me on at the café during the winter anyway. Are we done with shopping? I fancy going somewhere peaceful. Get some sea air.'

'Fine by me.'

Though they chatted pretty well non stop for the rest of the day, serious subjects were banned. They drove to Newquay and watched surfers riding stupidly large waves and ate ice creams. It was a glorious day and both of them felt relaxed.

In the evening, they went out for a lovely meal, which Jenny paid for, and went to find a club afterwards. It was so bad that they left early and went back to the apartment.

'Could you believe that DJ? He was almost as bad as the music he chose.'

'It has been fun though Jenny. I've been missing you. Missing seeing people outside work too. Thanks for coming down.'

'It's been a lovely little holiday for me. Much too short but well worth coming to see you in your Cornish hideaway.'

'You won't tell my parents where I am, will you?'

'Not if you don't want me to. I can hedge without telling them outright lies. So, what time is your dream man coming here tomorrow?' she asked with a grin.

'Oh heavens. I've still only got instant coffee.'

'Shouldn't worry. He'll probably never notice.'

'He's quite a coffee gourmet actually.'

'Make it strong and serve it in a jug. Always looks better.'

'I think I'm ready for bed. It's well after

midnight and we've been on the go all day.'

'Could it be that we're getting old? No stamina any more.'

'Awful thought but you could be right, Jenny. Night, love. And thanks again.'

As she lay in bed, Georgie pondered the advice. Jenny was right. Jay must be earning reasonable wages and yet he spent very little. Not that it was a problem. She didn't want money to be spent on her. What had happened? A few drinks together. One picnic and a number of rather passionate kisses. All her thoughts had been centred round him and the intense physical attraction. It certainly wasn't enough for her to give in to temptation and the consequences that might bring. No, she decided, she would enjoy his company when it was available and make sure she did other things instead of waiting for him to be free. She felt certain he was being less than honest and might well have someone else in his life. But it hurt so much to think of him with anyone else.

*   *   *

When she went into the sitting room, Jenny was already up and dressed and had folded the sofa bed away. She was sitting near the window, looking out at the sea.

'Morning. Hope you don't mind, I helped myself to coffee. I can see why you love this place. It's so peaceful.'

'I'm glad you like it. It certainly has compensations even if life is a bit too quiet at times. I think it was what I needed.'

'And Jay?'

'Him too. But I've thought about what you said. I shouldn't go too far with him. He can be a close friend and we can go out together but he isn't going to be my Mister Right. So, what do you want for breakfast? There's a choice of toast or toast.'

'I'll take the toast, thanks.'

At ten-thirty, right on time, the doorbell rang. Her heart missed a beat as she let him in. Jay was looking even more gorgeous after a few days of not seeing him. He rested an arm on her shoulder and bent to kiss her. She felt the urgency of need rush through her body as she kissed him back. She heard a sound behind her and swung round.

'Jenny. This is Jay. Jay, meet Jenny, my best friend.'

'Good to meet you,' he replied, taking her hand quite formally. Jenny seemed taken aback.

'Hi,' she murmured and even managed to blush slightly. 'Nice to meet you.'

'I'll get some coffee. Sit down and make yourselves at home.' Gina went to the small kitchen and began to spoon coffee into mugs.

'Hope you've had fun,' Jay said. 'All right for some, while I've been working my socks off.'

'Really?' Jenny said coolly.

'Very busy. Usually are on Saturdays. Seems to be the evening everyone goes out to eat. So, what did you two get up to yesterday?'

'Bit of retail therapy and a bit of sightseeing. Haven't you got any biscuits, Georgie?' Jenny asked as her friend arrived with the coffee.

She glared. Wrong name she mouthed.

'Georgie? I thought it was Gina?'

'Unfortunately, it's a name with any number of diminutives.'

'I rather like Georgie, actually. It suits you.'

'I feel it may be a bit childish really,' Georgie said, blushing.

Jenny looked embarrassed. 'Yes, I'm sorry. I forgot you were trying to be grown up. Gina it is, except when I forget. I've been calling you Georgie most of my life.' She smiled and took her coffee from the tray.

The conversation was slightly strained with both girls trying hard not to give anything away. Georgie hadn't realised how difficult it was going to be to mix the past she didn't want to remember with the future that was pretty uncertain.

'Are you on lunch duty today?' she asked.

'Afraid so. I'll have to go soon. Time to change into the black uniform and be polite to the masses. Sunday lunch is always something of a tradition in Cornwall. When can we meet again, Gina . . . or should it be Georgie?'

71

'You seem to be the one with commitments,' she replied with some hesitancy. She knew that she still wanted him like crazy, even after everything her friend had been saying.

'Tuesday evening? We could go to the cinema if you like?'

'Sounds good to me. Thanks.'

'I'll text to confirm the time. Good to meet you Jenny. Safe journey back.' He walked to the door, hesitating just before he opened it.

'Bye Gina. Nice to see your friend and even better to see you.' He pulled her close and kissed her very gently, tenderly. 'I can't wait until Tuesday. I curse my work for getting in the way of us.'

'Know what you mean. I'll see you then. Bye, love.'

She watched him walk away and went back to her friend.

'I can certainly see why you're tempted. He's gorgeous. Well fit, as they say.'

'I know. At least you can see my dilemma now. He seems so affectionate and he's everything I could dream of. He's spoiled anything I might ever have felt for Guy.'

'I can see that, but there is still the vexed question of why he said he was working on Friday when he was clearly coming back from somewhere, on a bus.'

'I know, you're right, but I have to keep remembering that I'm living a lie too. What will he do or say when he discovers who I really am?'

'It will be interesting to see. If he really doesn't know who you are, it's safe enough to assume he likes you for who you are. Has he seen your flashy little car yet? That might take some explaining. A waitress in a seaside café doesn't usually drive around in something that costs upwards of thirty grand.'

'I thought I'd say I won it in a competition,' she explained.

'You have become quite devious, haven't you?'

'I know. Fun, isn't it? And he doesn't suspect a thing. I hope he doesn't, anyway.'

'You're playing a dangerous game Georgie. Be careful.'

CHAPTER SIX

Georgie received several texts during the next two days. Their date for Tuesday evening was on and she offered to drive them both to the nearest town for their cinema outing.

'I needed to have the chance to kiss you before we go out,' he offered in explanation when he arrived at her apartment. 'It would have been embarrassing in front of the hotel. I've been missing you. I hated you being with someone else all weekend.'

'Don't be silly. It was my school friend Jenny, not some bloke,' she teased.

'I know. I'm just very frustrated that we can't spend more time together. There's something very special between us. You feel it too, don't you?'

'I think so, but we still don't know much about each other. Who we are, all the baggage.' She had thought about it so many times since Jenny's departure. Her friend had voiced everything she'd been worrying about, but his physical presence made all her doubts recede.

'I know you're right. I don't even know what music you like, what films or television. Mind you, I've lost touch with most television since I've been here.'

'Let's go and see if our taste in films coincides for a start.'

'Okay. So, where's this car of yours?'

'In the garage down below. Prepare yourself for a surprise.'

'What do you mean?'

'I don't know what you're expecting.'

'Nor do I. Something small and neat perhaps?'

'It's not large. It's quite neat, I suppose.'

'Can't wait. You've got me quite intrigued.'

She unlocked the garage and revealed her sports car. It was ice blue, sleek and obviously expensive. She didn't usually think twice about it but now, it seemed an exposure of her real self and her real life.

'Wow! That didn't come cheap,' Jay exclaimed. 'Is there something you should be telling me?'

'I won it in a sort of competition,' she lied. 'It's rather gorgeous, isn't it?'

'Very nice,' he agreed with a nod. 'But as you said, quite a surprise. I should think it's expensive to run and the insurance alone would eat most of my earnings.'

'Insurance was included,' she continued to fib. 'I haven't been using it much so the petrol's been okay so far. Let's go.'

Gina's long legs stretched under the dashboard; she was a confident driver and they soon left the village behind them.

'It goes like a dream, doesn't it? Perhaps a car like this is the next thing to add to my dream list. I can't believe you could win something like this. Lucky girl. Wow. What more could I want? A beautiful woman beside me and a car like this. I've died and gone to heaven.'

'It's just a car, Jay. I'd let you have a go but the insurance only covers me, I'm afraid.'

'I wouldn't dare to drive it anyway. I'm more used to a beaten up old banger. So, which film do you fancy?'

When the film started, Jay casually put his arm across the back of her seat and she had rested her head comfortably on his shoulder. It felt easy and familiar, though it was the

75

first time they had spent such an evening. At least he had paid for them both, she reflected, thinking about Jenny's comment that he was not very generous. As they drove back to Poltoon, she wondered how to deal with what might happen next.

'Do you want some coffee?' she asked.

'I'm not sure it's a good idea. Might be too tempting. I learned my lesson the last time,' he said with an easy grin.

'I'm sorry.'

'No worries, but I think it's best to decline the coffee. You're just too lovely for me to leave alone. We'll see each other again very soon. Promise. I'll call you.'

'Thank you for a lovely evening, Jay. It's been great.'

He reached over to kiss her and touched her cheek as he was getting out of the car. 'Night, my dear little Georgie. You don't mind, do you? Me using that name? It suits you so much better than Gina.'

'No, I don't mind. And I look forward to seeing you soon.'

He seemed to be understanding and mindful of her wishes. All plus points. It made her feel more comfortable, as she reflected on Jenny's advice. She could easily convince herself that Jenny didn't have all the right answers. There were things going on in Jay's life, things he hadn't spoken of, but she still wanted him, very much.

Things came to a head a few days later. They took the bus out to a pub along the coast and ate hot pasties and drank beer. When they arrived back at Georgie's apartment, Jay went inside with her.

'You're driving me wild, Georgie Hind.' He drew her close and kissed her until they both felt dizzy with joy, desire, all the feelings she had ever read about in her favourite romances. Now she really knew what it felt like to be properly in love.

'I love you Jay,' she whispered.

'Oh my darling. I've longed for you to say that. I fell in love with you just seconds after I saw you. In that ridiculous little cap you wear at work. I wanted to snatch it off and let your gorgeous hair fall down, like it is now.' He was stroking her hair, touching her neck and sending shivers of delight coursing through her body. Very gently, he cupped her face in his hands and kissed every inch of her face.

'I want you Jay,' she whispered hoarsely.

'Are you sure?' he whispered.

She nodded, taking his hand.

*   *   *

Her alarm rang at seven o'clock the next morning. The pair jolted awake and Jay reached for his watch.

'Oh heavens, I'm late. I have breakfast duties starting in less than ten minutes.' He flung back the duvet and rushed into her shower. He tugged on his clothes, kissed her perfunctorily on the nose and rushed out of the apartment. She smiled and looked up the hill, seeing him running towards the hotel at top speed. She hugged the duvet close to her and stretched again. She felt languid and still sleepy.

'You look happy,' Audrey told her when she arrived at work later. 'Nice evening?'

'Great, thanks. Are you okay? You look a bit pale.'

'To tell you the truth, I'm not feeling the best today. I'm wondering if I'm coming down with something.'

'I can do things here. You take it easy. I'm sure I know the routine well enough now. Why don't you go and rest and I'll do the scones and get the lunch things ready while we're quiet.'

'That's good of you, dear. I think I'll go back home if that's all right and maybe take something. Give me a buzz when you need me.' She went through the back door of the kitchen area to her house, across the yard. There was an intercom between the two so it was easy to contact each other without leaving the place unattended.

Happily, Georgie made scones, wiped over the tables and prepared dishes of jam and cream ready to serve. She even had the coffee machine primed and ready to switch on when customers arrived.

She glanced around for the next thing to do and realised the salad and quiches needed preparing for lunch. Humming, she quickly organised everything, thanking her father for giving her such a thorough grounding in every aspect of the business. She rather enjoyed being in charge. It made her push away the enormity of what had happened last night. Jenny would be surprised at the way things had turned out. She would still keep it to herself and enjoy the thoughts for a while.

Lunchtime proved rather hectic, serving, making up sandwiches and rolls to order and keeping on top of the clearing up. She was determined to manage and let Audrey recover. Hopefully, a day off would make her feel better. Once the tea rush was over, Georgie had time to catch up with the washing up. For the first time, she had a moment to remember what had happened the previous evening. Her heart gave a twist at the thought and she finished her work with a silly grin on her face.

She now felt she was truly an adult and had finally escaped from her parents' control. She wanted to shout it from the rooftops, tell everyone she was in love. Maybe she had been foolish, but she felt euphoric and nothing was going to spoil her joyous mood.

She locked the front door and went through to knock on Audrey's door. After some while, the woman came to the door.

'I suspect it's a bout of summer flu. I feel

terrible. Everything aches—I think we'll have to close tomorrow. I'm sorry but I can't think straight.'

'I can manage. I did okay today. It was a bit of a rush at lunchtime but if I cut down on what we serve, I'm happy to manage it all. I'll cash up, shall I and bring the takings over? I didn't like to do it without asking.'

'If you're sure. I'd be most grateful. Do you know how to check off the till roll and everything? If not, bring it all over and Charlie will do it when he comes home.'

'Of course. I'll do it all.'

'You'll find some cash bags in the box under the counter.'

'Don't worry. Get back inside and I'll see you soon. Would you like me to make you a hot drink when I'm finished?'

'I'm okay thanks love. I do appreciate it.' She swayed on her feet, looking as if she was about to collapse.

Georgie quickly sorted out the cash. It was a simple method and much less technical than any of their hotel systems. She packed coins and notes into cash bags and took it over with the paper reconciliation. It was all clear and straightforward. She even took the pot where tips were left, usually shared between them at the end of the week. Once she had checked the fridge and freezer for the supplies for the next day, she locked up and went back to her apartment, taking the key with her.

Jay had sent a couple of texts which she hadn't even read, let alone replied to.

Can I come to your place later this evening? Miss you! J xx

How much later?

When I finish? Ten-ish?

I'll be waiting xx

She grinned to herself and hugged her arms round her body. Life was brilliant. She cooked herself some eggs and ate some fruit that looked as if it had seen better days. Her phone rang. It was her mother.

'Hello, Mummy. How are you?'

'I'm fine. But how are you? I'm so worried about you.'

'Don't be. Everything is going really well and I'm loving what I'm doing.'

'I'm afraid I have some bad news. Daddy says he's refused to pay your credit card. Obviously you've been using it for rent and petrol. Have you got some money? Can you manage on what you're earning? I don't want you going hungry or being short of cash. You're not used to managing, are you?'

'Well, no, I suppose not. Daddy's always organised my finances, but I still have some money in the bank and I'll find somewhere cheaper to live.'

'I can let you have a cheque if you need it, darling. No need to say anything to your father. Can't you tell me where you are and what you're doing?'

'Please don't ask, Mummy. You know what will happen. Daddy will come roaring down and demand I go back and I'm actually having a really good time.' If only she knew, she thought with a slight grimace.

'Well . . . if you're sure, but I wanted to warn you. He won't pay the last credit card bill that came in. Says if you want to be independent then you have to pay it yourself. It was over a thousand pounds. Have you got that?'

'I think so,' she said with a gulp, knowing that paying it would clean her out, especially after the weekend with Jenny when she'd had her shopping spree. She didn't even know how to pay a credit card bill. 'So what do I have to do?'

'I'm not sure. I suppose you'd have to send a cheque. It's usually paid automatically from Daddy's account. I'll find the bill and let you know.'

'Thanks, Mummy. Text me the details, I'll sort it out. I hope you aren't getting too much hassle from him, are you?'

'I'm coping. I do miss you though. When might we see you?'

'I'm not sure. Please don't worry about me. Thanks for phoning, Mummy.'

It was certainly a blow. She had planned to stay another week in this apartment but now, all her savings would go on paying for the previous month. She had a few days left to look for somewhere else.

She went to look at the cards in the post office window. Apart from a caravan, which still seemed rather expensive, there was nothing suitable. Perhaps she would have to look inland but she would then have to travel in to work each day and pay for car parking on top. Why did this have to happen now, just when things were going so well? She wouldn't say anything to Jay. Not yet any way.

Jay arrived just after ten o'clock, as promised.

'I'm shattered,' he announced, 'but I couldn't bear not to see you. I had to leave so quickly this morning and I wanted to see that you were okay. And I thought I might stay over again . . . if that's all right?'

'Of course. Do you want a drink? I've got some wine or a soft drink. Or coffee.'

'Wine sounds wonderful.'

'Might as well make the most of it. I'm going to have to move out of here in a day or two. Can't afford it any longer.' Damn, she told herself. I wasn't going to say anything.

'That's a shame. I was thinking of asking if I could move in with you for a while.'

'If only . . .' she breathed, slightly terrified at the thought but equally, thinking it would be paradise.

'I could help out a bit with rent but not very much really. You know my situation.'

'I'd love you to but I haven't found anywhere else yet. I might have to move away from the village but even that means more expense with travelling and parking.'

'Just when I thought we were getting ourselves sorted.'

'We'll just have to make the most of the next few days . . . and evenings. Audrey is ill so I'm running things single handed at the café for a while.'

'Heavens. Can you do it?'

'Course I can, but it's a bit hectic at times.'

'Don't let her take advantage of you.'

'Of course she wouldn't. But she is quite unwell so I may be on my own for a while. How was your day?'

'Not bad. I was late this morning but it wasn't a problem. One of the girls covered for me. I had a couple of hours off during the day and then it was all go again this evening. Thanks for letting me come round so late. I've brought a few toiletries with me so I can be more organised in the morning.'

Georgie awoke first and watched as Jay gradually roused. There was something very intimate about watching someone sleeping. His face looked so peaceful and the clean lines and strong jaw line were things she would never tire of seeing. His black hair was rumpled and fell as soft curls over his forehead. He opened his eyes and grinned.

'I could enjoy waking up like this every day,' he murmured. 'What's the time?'

'Six-thirty.'

'Good. Not such a rush then. Come here.' He drew her close and kissed her soft lips. 'That's as much as I dare do now, but thank you for being you and letting me share a little part of you.'

'Thank you for caring. Now, be off with you and get yourself ready for work.'

She made coffee and toast and handed it to him when he came out of the shower.

'Thank you but you didn't have to do that. I get a proper breakfast when the guests have all been fed.'

'I wanted to do it. Can't have you going out without even a cup of coffee.' It felt comfortable and homely.

'I was thinking,' he began. 'I could ask at the hotel if they'd allow you to stay in the caravan with me. It's meant for two people to share so there's room. I'm just not sure they will allow someone to move in who's not working at the hotel.'

'That would be amazing. Perhaps I could work a shift on reception or something during the evening when you're working.'

'Leave it with me. Do you have any experience of working on a reception desk?'

Did she have experience? She almost laughed out loud. She'd been doing far more than that for the last few years. There wasn't a system in existence she hadn't looked at.

'Oh yes. I could manage that quite easily,' she replied.

'They'd need a CV and details of experience and references of course.'

'I'm not sure about that. I'd ask Audrey but I doubt that would count for much.'

'We'll talk more later. Better dash now. Bye Georgie. I should be able to get away earlier tonight. I can come here again?'

'Course you can. I'll look forward to it.'

*   *   *

Audrey was no better and Georgie was met at the shop door by Charlie, her husband.

'I'm sorry but it may be better to close today. Audrey needs her rest and it isn't fair to leave you on your own.'

'I really don't mind. I managed yesterday and I'm happy to do it again today. I may not put on quite so many lunch dishes but I can do sandwiches and rolls. Besides, the deliveries are already here. Don't want to waste things.' She pointed to the trays of rolls and bread left in their usual place.

'Well, if you're sure, but I don't want Audrey to be disturbed if things don't work out. We can't even get the extra girls in as they're still at school.'

'It's okay. I'll manage.'

'Well, thank you very much. We'll make it up to you. A bit of a bonus.'

'Thank you. I appreciate it. Now, I'd better get going. Scones first, I think.'

She worked quickly and soon had everything organised. She enjoyed being in charge, alone. It allowed her thinking space and time to relish the new phase her life had entered. When she finally told Jay who she really was, their lives together could really take shape.

The odd absences, bus trips and even the possibility of someone else in his life had all been forgotten. Now he'd suggested that they should move in together, it made everything all right.

He arrived at eight o'clock that evening. She was expecting him and with Audrey's permission, had brought some food home for their supper. It was a simple selection of salads and cooked meats, followed by strawberries bought from the grocer nearby.

'That was lovely. Thank you,' he said when the plates were all empty. 'I'll help with the washing up and then we can relax. It's great being together like this. Well, I think so anyway.'

'Feels a bit like being a married couple, doesn't it?' He straightened and looked at her with a strange expression she didn't understand. 'Sorry, have I said something wrong?'

'No. Of course not, Georgie. It was the word 'married' that startled me.'

'Sorry. I didn't mean anything by it,' she blustered. 'I wasn't even thinking of the implications. It's just perfect, that's all.'

'Of course,' he replied but she could see that he felt uneasy. She was struck by a dreadful thought. Suppose he was already married? He certainly had a great deal more experience than she did. He'd been slightly shocked to discover that he was her first partner. She shrank away from the thought.

'Did you ask about me moving in with you?' she asked, her voice a little quieter than usual.

'The manager who deals with it wasn't in today. I'll try again tomorrow, but you can always come for a night or two. At least it means you won't have to worry.'

'I'll have to bring my car. The garage goes with this place.'

'I'm sure it will be fine. Now, come and sit down. Let's watch something silly on television.'

They sat side by side on the sofa, his arm round her and she rested her head against him.

'I can hear your heart beating,' she murmured. 'A good steady pace.' She nestled closer and felt his heartbeat quicken in response.

'We could always have an early night instead of watching this drivel,' he whispered.

'I agree,' she said, taking his hand. 'It's total drivel.'

*   *   *

By the end of the week, Audrey was improving

and insisted on coming into work on the Friday afternoon. She told Georgie to take a couple of hours off the next morning, once she heard that she was moving out of the apartment.

'So where are you going?'

'Actually, I'm moving in with Jay.' She was slightly hesitant, not knowing quite how Audrey would take it. She was a bit strait-laced and might not approve of the situation, but she took it well.

'If it doesn't work out, we have a spare room and you could always stay with us. We don't have a garage though, so you'd have to find somewhere to leave your car.'

'That's so kind of you. I'm hoping it will work out. Jay thinks it will be okay. I was actually thinking of seeing if they have any evening vacancies to make it legitimate. You wouldn't object, would you?'

'Well . . . not really. As long as you don't wear yourself out. It's quite busy here in the summer months.'

'I'll be fine. But I'll be glad of the time off to clean the apartment. I'm supposed to vacate by ten o'clock. I'm moving some of my stuff this evening. Good job there isn't too much.'

She thought of her massive walk in wardrobe at home and cringed at the thought of the amount of clothes she had there. She was becoming quite used to this minimalist style of living. At least she didn't have to decide what to wear.

'If you're sure you can manage, I'll come in about eleven, in good time for the lunch rush.'

'That'll be fine,' Audrey told her. 'They do have people to go in and clean before the next tenants arrive, you know. Is there someone moving straight in?'

'I don't think so. I was going to renew but decided it's really more than I can afford. It's been lovely though.'

'Well, I hope it all works out for you. He's a handsome chap, I must say. You make an attractive couple.'

'Thank you. You should go and rest now while I finish off. I've just got to wipe down the surfaces and cash up.'

'I'll do the till if you like. Save you coming across with it.'

'If you feel up to it. Thanks. I think everything is in order.'

'You seem to know your way around everything very well. Have you done this sort of work before?' her boss enquired.

'Well, something similar.'

'And you managed this whole place on your own without a problem. Look, I have something to put to you. I've been thinking I'd like to retire soon. How would you feel about managing this place on a permanent basis? It would be a salaried position and all the year round, of course. You'd be able to find somewhere to live and really settle down.'

Georgie gasped. She certainly hadn't seen

that one coming and wasn't entirely sure what to say without appearing rude.

'I'm very flattered of course, but I don't know what my plans are in the long term.'

'Well, think about it. The offer's there. It's a good place to live and I have every confidence you could manage it however you'd like to. I wouldn't interfere if you wanted to make changes. It would be up to you. Perhaps your young man would think of making it a proper partnership. He's a waiter, I understand.'

'Well, yes, but that's just for the season. He'll be going to college soon.'

'I see. Well, I'm in no hurry for your answer. I'm not planning to hang up my apron yet. I hope you know what you're doing. What do your parents think?'

'I haven't told them yet. They'd be shocked though, I'm sure,' she admitted.

She dreaded to think what her parents would say, if they ever found out. But it was what she wanted to do, whatever happened in the future.

CHAPTER SEVEN

At the end of the day Georgie went back to her apartment and regretfully packed up her things. She felt slightly sad to be leaving her haven but the prospect of being with Jay overrode everything else.

She watched for him at the window but by nine o'clock there was still no sign of him. She saw the service bus coming in and watched the passengers getting off. She stared and blinked slightly. There was Jay, once more getting off the bus when he'd said he was working. He glanced around and headed towards her apartment.

Should she ask him where he'd been? Or wait for him to say something? She heard him running up the stairs and went to open the door.

'Sorry. I was a bit later than I intended. Something came up.'

'Oh yes? Extra customers needing you?'

'Something like that. Have you eaten?'

'I finished up some bits left in the fridge. How about you?'

'I got something earlier. So, it looks as if you're all set for the move then?'

'I've packed up most of my stuff. I hope it will all fit in. Are you sure it's okay if I move in?'

'No problem. Do you want to take anything up tonight? Or shall we leave it and enjoy our last night here?'

'I've got some time off tomorrow. My reward for working hard all week. Audrey is better so she'll be back in the kitchen. Oh yes, she actually offered me a permanent job as manager of the place. She wants to retire.

Said I'd have a free hand to run it however I wanted.'

'Wow! Congratulations. Will you take up the offer?'

'No, of course not. I don't see a small seaside café as my future, somehow . . .'

'So what do you see as your future?'

Georgie hesitated. Her future was taking over the Hetherington Hotel chain as chief executive, once her father retired, whenever that might be. The Beach Café, Poltoon could hardly compete. This was her temporary job to give her time and space. Mind you, she thought, that was before Jay had swept into her life.

'I'm not sure what I'm going to do, but this is just a sort of breathing space for me.'

'You scarcely mention your family. Do they approve of what you're doing?'

'No. They're furious with me, but I refuse to be ordered around by them, told what to do and how to do it all the time . . . My father seems to think his is the only way to do anything,' she confessed.

'Well now, that's the most you've ever said about them. I take it you were working with him?'

Georgie was entering dangerous territory. Her carefully guarded cover was slipping.

'I was working in the family . . . family firm.'

'What sort of business?' Jay asked curiously.

'I really don't want to talk about it. Let's

enjoy what's left of the evening.'

'If that's what you want.'

They both fell silent for a few moments. Georgie was fighting with her desire to come clean about who she was and at the same time, desperately wanting to ask about his trips on the bus. It seemed neither of them was being completely honest.

She didn't have the right to ask him when she was keeping her own secrets. Perhaps it was just a summer fling and she should leave it at that. Come August, she would have to decide when and how she was going to return home and get on with the rest of her life. The trouble was, she couldn't envisage any sort of life that didn't include Jay. She wanted him to be a part of her future. She wanted him to be welcomed into her family and their empire. She might even include marriage in her pipe dreams. Once more her dreaded nightmare hit her . . . unless he was already married.

'So, you've had girlfriends before. Anyone special I should hear about?' she asked, trying to lighten the words with a smile.

'Where did that come from?'

'You're obviously much more experienced than I am. I was wondering if I have a rival.'

His face clouded and his eyes flashed dangerously.

'That's not a nice thing to say. What sort of person do you think I am?'

'I'm sorry, but I can't help wondering. You

seem to be working ridiculous hours but you are very short of money. I could be suspicious about why.'

'How could you think so badly of me?' He broke away from her and stood up. He was looking more and more angry. 'I don't like the way this is going. What exactly are you suspicious of? Something's set you off on this track.'

In for a pound, she thought.

'I've seen you getting off the bus several times when you said you'd been working. And I thought saw you at the cinema once, with a dark haired girl.'

Jay's face looked like thunder. He was ready to explode.

'Well, I'm sorry if I don't tell you every single thing I do any more than you tell me. I'm not even going to reply to your comments. Are you sure you actually want to move in with me and the hoard of other women I hide in the wardrobes?'

'I'm sorry Jay. I'm really sorry. I don't know why I said it. We both have a past and we both deserve some privacy.'

He turned towards her again and the anger melted from his face. He held out his hands towards her and she went to him. He kissed her tenderly and she smiled up at him. Looking into his eyes when they were angry had scared her but now they were hazy with . . . well, was it love?

'Sorry,' they both murmured together.

*   *   *

Jay left early to do his breakfast shift and they arranged that he would meet her at nine-thirty at the hotel.

She loaded her car until it was nearly impossible to drive. She cleaned round the apartment, wiping down shelves and making it all as pristine as when she moved in. When it was done, she stood by the window, watching the families gathering on the beach. It was windy and not very pleasant but still people gravitated towards the sea. It was something about being on holiday that made everyone think they must enjoy it, even when the weather was bad.

Georgie glanced at her watch. Nine-fifteen. Just about time to move and begin the next phase of her life. This was quite some move. She was putting herself into a situation where she was reliant on someone else. Someone who had secrets, just as she did. What happened if it didn't work out? There was always Audrey's offer if necessary.

Living with someone this way was something entirely new to her and though it was a risk, it was exactly the sort of risk she had wanted.

She locked the door and went down the stairs. She took the keys to the office and left them with the receptionist.

'Hope you've enjoyed your stay. Do we have your address in case of any queries?'

'Oh, er no, but I shall be working in the Beach Café for a while longer. You can contact me there.'

'Okay. Thanks. Just a case of checking the inventory. I'm sure you've left things as we would expect.'

'I hope so. No breakages and nothing damaged. I left the sheets in the basket as instructed. Right. I'd better move.'

'Can I ask why you're vacating, if you're still working here?'

'I'm afraid it's too expensive for me with the rise in rentals for the summer season.'

'I'm sure we could have come to an arrangement for a long term tenancy.'

'Even so, it was more than I can pay. Thanks anyway. Is it let this week?'

'No. Not for two more weeks.'

'Ah well. Too late now. I've settled on somewhere else.'

She went to her car and drove up the hill to the Clarence Hotel for the first time. She was filled with nervous anticipation. Jenny would certainly think she was crazy and her parents would be furious. But, she reasoned, if she'd been away at university, who knows what would have happened there? Student life certainly had a reputation.

There was a row of caravans to one side of the main buildings. She saw Jay come round, presumably from the kitchen area.

'Hello again, you. If you park next to this one, we can unload and then you'll have to move the car round to one side. Everything okay?'

'Yes, I think so. Handed the keys back. Looks a nice caravan. I've never been in one before.'

'It's not bad. Reasonable amount of space but tidiness is essential or you keep falling over everything. Welcome.'

'Thank you.'

Georgie felt unexpectedly shy as she went up the steps. The sitting room was surprisingly spacious with a tiny galley kitchen to one side. There was a fridge and cooker and several cupboards for storing crockery and cooking utensils. Jay showed them to her as they passed.

'I rarely do any cooking as we mostly eat in the hotel but I expect we shall want to eat together. Now, the bedroom's through here. It officially divides into two but I've been leaving the screens open to give more space.'

The room was filled with the large double bed and the single bed on the other side was used for storage.

'I've cleared this half of the wardrobe. Hope that will give you enough space. There're some lockers under the single bed to store shoes and things, and there's a drawer for you in this unit. Bathroom—or shower room, more correctly—is this one.'

He opened what she thought was a cupboard, to reveal a tiny compartment with a shower and toilet and small hand sink. Compact was a generous word for it.

'Fine,' Georgie gulped, trying not to look shocked. 'It's good of you to share your space.'

'I'm delighted you want to share it. Come here. Welcome to our first home together, such as it is.' He drew her close and kissed her, holding her as if he couldn't believe his luck.

'Oh Jay. I hope this all works out. I'm very excited. I need to unpack as I have to get to work in the next half hour.'

'We'll load everything into the little room for now. I'm on the lunch shift too and then I have a few hours off. I start again at eight so you'll have the evening to unpack and sort things out and I can help you later.'

*   *   *

It seemed a very peculiar day. Serving meals, washing up and generally doing her job seemed a million miles from the enormity of moving in with Jay. Her world was shrinking fast. Her wardrobe at home was about the size of this entire caravan. She walked wearily back up the hill, knowing that Jay would be waiting for her. He wouldn't be able to make his mysterious bus journeys any more without her knowing.

'Come and sit down. You must be worn out.'

'Well, I am. But you are too and you have an evening of work ahead as well.'

'I want you to feel at home. I know it must be difficult for you but I hope you'll soon settle. It's your place now, too. Oh, and I did ask about job vacancies. They need some relief cover. They want two references. Character references mostly. I thought Audrey might be willing and someone else you've worked for.'

'I've worked with Jenny before. Maybe she would do.'

'Give it a try anyway. It will only be a few hours here and there, but at least that way they can't object about you staying in the caravan.'

It took them a few days to settle. Georgie had persuaded Jenny to write a professional looking reference and she even used the pseudonym. Georgie avoided telling her friend that she had moved in with Jay, but it had been her own decision.

She worked the reception for the first time the following Monday. She was shown the system by the main receptionist.

'Mondays are usually pretty quiet so you shouldn't have any problems. The duty manager will be around if you have any queries, though.'

'Thank you,' Georgie said politely. The system was rather an old one compared to the Hetherington but was adequate for the size of hotel. She was familiar with it and in any case, it was unlikely she would be required to do anything complicated.

Jay came to the desk during the evening. 'How's it going?'

'It's fine. No problems. It's an easy system and all I have to do really is answer the phone and smile at people.'

'You do that beautifully. As long as you keep plenty of smiles for me. What time do you finish?'

'Ten-thirty.'

'I'll come and join you then. I like the snazzy uniform. Suits you. You look very efficient sitting there with your hair all tied back. I shall look forward to letting it loose again.'

'Get back to work before I leap over the counter and harass you.' She laughed.

'Now there's a threat that sounds better than a promise. See you soon.'

The rest of the evening was quiet. She looked up as a party of guests came from the dining room. She half listened to their conversation but took little notice.

'Been good to see you again. Perhaps you'd like to join us for dinner at our hotel later in the week? It's The Hetherington, in a village near St Austell.'

'That's a nice idea. We might do that.'

Georgie cringed and lowered her head. She tried to see if it was anyone she knew, without letting herself be seen.

'Georgina? It is you. What are you doing here?'

'Oh, hello. I'm just seeing what the competition are doing. Checking out the system, you know the sort of thing.' She recognised the acquaintance of her father and smiled politely.

'How are the family?'

'Fine thanks.' To her great relief, the phone rang. She excused herself and answered it. She raised a hand in a farewell gesture as she dealt with the call. She felt herself blushing furiously and hoped that he and his wife didn't meet her father any time soon.

It still felt strange to leave her working day behind and share her evening with someone else. Strange but exciting. In the few days she had been there, it had been pleasure all the way.

The only difficult thing to deal with had been settling her credit card bill. Her mother had sent the details and she had been able to pay it at the local bank. It had all but cleaned her out. The extra cash she would earn at the hotel would be most welcome. At least her living costs were cheaper and she should manage for the next few weeks.

Disaster struck a few days later, though. She awoke one morning, feeling ill. She must have caught a stomach bug and it was hitting her badly. Though Jay was sympathetic, he didn't know what to do and left her while he worked.

Health and safety rules meant she was not allowed to work until the bug had cleared for several days. She felt terrible about leaving Audrey in the lurch. To make matters worse, Jay asked her for some cash towards the rental of the caravan—she was somewhat surprised as she'd assumed it was part of his wages.

'I'm sorry love but I do have to pay for it. Okay, it's not a lot, but I'm a bit short of cash this week. I had to pay off some bills. I'm sorry to ask but I'm in a bit of a hole.'

'I'm sorry but I can't. I also had to pay off some bills and I'm completely cleaned out until I get paid. With not working this week, I won't get anything anyway.'

He looked angry and started to say something but stopped himself. Georgie was looking very pale and was clearly unwell and he didn't want to add to her misery.

'I'm sorry. I'm not sure what to do. I shouldn't have asked, especially when you're feeling ill. But can't you pretend it was a false alarm and go back to work anyway?'

'I mustn't. Suppose I still have some sort of bug and pass it on to the customers? Audrey could be closed down. It's always in the news about cafés and restaurants being closed.'

He stormed off, looking angry and she flopped back onto the bed. She'd thought he was saving for his course and was confused to hear that he was so short of money. She wondered where his wages had gone. She thought again about his mysterious visits to . . . to wherever it was.

She hated the doubts and tried to dismiss them. She felt certain that he did love her. He said it often enough but there were so many things she didn't know.

Whatever happened, she refused to ask her parents for money. It came hard, having to think about money all the time. It was a totally new experience for her.

She tried to focus on other things and decided she felt well enough for a gentle stroll. As she left the caravan she met Jay returning after his breakfast shift.

'Are you all right?' he asked.

'Just felt like getting some fresh air. A little walk along the top of the cliffs.'

'I'll come too. Look, I'm sorry I had to ask for money. I'll ask the manager for an advance on my wages for next month.'

'But won't that mean you'll be short the following month?'

'Maybe, but I'll just have to save more, won't I?'

'Maybe there will be more tips when there are more holidaymakers. After that it will be back to college, won't it?'

'I suppose so. Not entirely sure though. Things change. What would you do if I go to college?'

'Haven't thought. Where will you be living?'

'I'll have to find a bedsit or digs or

something. It's expensive living near Truro so I'm not sure.'

'I see.' Georgie's heart plummeted. Clearly Jay was thinking of himself. Whatever he decided to do, she was not included in his plans. So, even though they had both declared their love for each other, he obviously considered it to be just a holiday romance and nothing more.

How could she have been so stupid? She had let her emotions run away with *her* good sense.

CHAPTER EIGHT

After the weekend, Georgie went back to work. The Saturday girl was now on school holidays and so they were sharing the tasks. It meant more time off but less money.

Audrey had repeated the offer for Georgie to take over as manager but she had firmly turned it down. It wasn't the future she wanted. She had been feeling desperate for a few days, knowing that her future with Jay was limited.

He kept asking her what was wrong but she couldn't tell him. She suffered in silence. Her unhappiness was made worse by more of Jay's absences. He never told her where he was going or why. She withdrew into herself and forced herself not to ask. Was she being stupid? If they were living together, surely he should confide in her?

She imagined many things, some worse than others. Her insecurity was growing. Two more weeks and the August bank holiday would bring an end to the season and her life with Jay. He would be leaving and the caravan and their temporary home would be shut up for the winter. However spacious it was for a caravan, it was still a rather confined area and there were times when they had been annoyed with each other for leaving things in the wrong places—but arguments were usually an excuse to make up again.

For several mornings recently, Georgie had woken feeling unwell. She assumed it was a recurrence of the bug she had suffered but later in the day, she felt fine again. It took her a couple of weeks to realise that her period was late. She gasped. How could she have been so utterly stupid? They hadn't taken proper precautions at the start of their relationship but surely she couldn't be pregnant, could she?

She sat on the side of the bed and began to shake. She felt very close to tears. What on earth would Jay say? He'd said nothing more about his future plans, which she now knew didn't include her. She let the tears fall unchecked. Jay was away doing his breakfast shift and she was due to go to the café. She glanced at her watch. She needed advice and decided to try and catch Jenny.

'Hello you. This is a bit early in the morning, isn't it? What's wrong?' Jenny's voice sounded comforting already.

'I'm in a terrible mess Jenny. I think I might be pregnant.' There was a long pause.

'Oh Georgie, don't tell me you were daft enough to have unprotected sex! When did this happen?'

'Ages ago. We're living together now. I couldn't afford to keep the apartment and I moved in with Jay to his caravan.'

'And what does he think about it?'

'I haven't told him. I've only just realised I'm late and I've been feeling unwell in the mornings.'

'So you haven't done a test?'

'No. I needed to speak to someone—a friend.'

'You are such an idiot. Get a pregnancy test and make sure. But he will stick by you, won't he?'

'I don't know. In fact, I don't know what will happen even without a baby in the mix. He's talking of going back to college soon and says he'll have to get a bedsit. Where does that leave me, Jenny?'

'You poor thing. Do you want me to come down again?'

'It would be great but there's nowhere for you to stay. The caravan is very cosy to say the least. My parents will be even more furious.

Don't say anything to them.'

'Course not. But you need to make proper plans. It's ridiculous to struggle on without money when you've got so much behind you.'

'I know but . . . I'll do as you say. Get a test first of all. I'll keep you posted.'

'Take care love and don't do anything stupid.'

'Thanks Jenny.'

She turned off her phone and decided she just had time to go and buy her test kit before work. She went out to the car park area. She looked around and couldn't see her car. Certain she had left it in the usual place, she walked, a little way but it was nowhere in sight. She was holding her keys in her hand so it hadn't been stolen. Maybe the spare set were missing? She went back inside and looked for them but without success. Could Jay have borrowed the car? He wouldn't have done so without asking. She ran through the main entrance and into the dining room. Jay was there and looked round at her in surprise.

'What's up? You look terrible.'

'The car. It's gone. I wondered if you'd borrowed it?'

He looked shocked. 'As if I'd ever do that. I'm amazed you'd even think I could. Were you going out somewhere?'

'Just to get some shopping.' The shock of her missing car had overtaken her anxiety about a possible pregnancy. 'I'd better call the police.'

'Give me a minute and I'll come with you. Let's look around first in case it's been moved or something.'

'The spare set of keys has gone. Someone must have taken them. Did you leave the door unlocked at any time?'

'I don't know. Must have done I suppose. Dammit. Hang on. I'll see if I can leave now and help you sort it out.'

He dashed into the kitchen and returned a few minutes later, having changed out of his waiter's uniform. 'Right. Come on.' He grabbed her hand and almost dragged her outside. They rushed round the various hotel car parking areas and looked down towards the village but there was no sign of the shiny blue sports car.

'I'm going to call the police, Jay. I have to. It's a very expensive car.'

'I know it is. I'm sorry love. I never heard anything in the night. I suppose you're sure it was there yesterday?'

'Well of course it was. I think it was. We'd have noticed if it wasn't, surely?'

'I suppose so. The hotel isn't going to like this. They won't like a police presence. Doesn't look good to the guests.'

'Hang the hotel. I'm not losing my car without someone doing something about it. I'm going to call the police right now.'

'I'd better go and tell the manager. Come

with me and we'll see what he says.'

'I don't understand you, Jay. It's almost as if you don't want me to call the police.'

'Don't be silly. I just know that they hate having any police on site.' He went back inside and headed to the desk, asking to see the manager.

The manager couldn't have been more obliging. 'Of course you must report the loss. Ask them to be discreet. In fact, I'll put in the call myself. Come into the office, both of you.' He made his report, asking Georgie to supply the car's number. 'You'd better contact your insurance company too. I assume you've got the papers and certificate safe?'

'I think so.'

'Don't tell me you left them inside the car?'

'Well no. I don't think I did. I know I always used to, till my father told me off for doing it. I'll check.'

'I'll send the police straight round to your caravan when they get here.'

'Thank you,' she said, leaving the office with her heart thumping in a most unpleasant way. This was the last thing she needed right now.

'It'll be all right. Just wait and see,' Jay tried to comfort her. 'I'm here for you.'

In truth, she wanted to see the police on her own. Her father had paid for the insurance and it was all in her real name. Her silly fib about winning the car in a competition was about to be exposed. How had she got herself into this stupid mess in the first place? With everything else that was happening, she had dug herself into an enormous hole. If Jay left her, as it looked as if he might anyway, she only had herself to blame.

'You go back to work. I can manage, thanks. I'll look out the papers and wait for the police to get here.'

'Don't be silly. I'm staying right here beside you.'

'I suppose you couldn't pop down to Audrey's and tell her I won't be there for a while?' she asked desperately.

'Phone her. She'll understand.'

'I was thinking you could do me the biggest favour and help her out if necessary.'

'Won't she have the Saturday girl there?'

'Not today. It was my turn to do the morning and she was coming in later.'

'Well, if you really think it's necessary, I'll go.' He sounded distinctly dubious.

'I'd be very grateful. Thanks.' He went away and she rummaged feverishly for the documents. At least on this occasion he wasn't going to find out her name. But, clearly she would have to confess quite soon. They both had secrets and it was time the air was cleared.

She touched her stomach and frowned. If there was indeed a baby in there, she needed to know soon and decide what was going to happen. She looked out of the window and saw the police car coming into the village and up

111

the hill towards her. She went outside to greet them.

Efficiently, they took down the details and description of the car. The younger officer looked at the caravan and pulled a face.

'This is where you're living? It's a rather expensive car for someone living in a caravan, isn't it?'

'It was present from my father. Twenty-first birthday.'

'Lucky you. Wish my father gave me that sort of present. Have you contacted your insurance company?'

'Not yet. I was waiting for you first.'

'This will be the report number,' he said, handing her a slip of paper. Give that to them and depending on your policy type, it might entitle you to a courtesy car while we try to track it down. It's pretty distinctive so it may be found quite quickly. These things are sometimes stolen to order. In that case, they'll change the number plates and re-spray it.'

'Heavens.'

'I think you mentioned the spare set of keys may have been taken. I suppose they were inside, were they?'

'Well yes. We think someone must have got in when the door was unlocked.'

'That could be a problem with the insurers. We'll be in touch as soon as we hear anything.'

'Thank you. You have my mobile number, don't you?' He nodded and they drove away without any further questions.

Georgie dialled the insurance company and gave them the details. After a great deal of thought, she phoned her mother. Her father's name was on the policy so he needed to know.

'Oh Georgie, how dreadful for you. We'll drive down right away. You don't have to deal with this alone. Daddy's intending to visit the Cornish Hetherington anyway, so we can be with you by this evening.'

'No, Mummy. Please don't. I'll be fine.'

'But how can you get around? Where are you exactly?'

'I'm fine. The police are dealing with it. I only told you because the insurance company will be in contact with Daddy. I don't need you fussing.'

'Oh Georgie, please. Be sensible. Tell me where you are.'

'I'm fine, Mummy. Thank you. Pass the message on.' She switched off the phone and sent up a little prayer that her parents didn't turn up on the doorstep. Moments later, Jay arrived back.

'Audrey says she'll manage. We're free till lunchtime. Now, what's to be done? I saw the police car driving off.'

'Nothing's to be done. Just a matter of waiting, I'm afraid.'

'Okay. So what shopping do we need? We can go to the shops now if you like.'

'Nothing that matters. I just wanted some

fruit.' She gathered up the insurance papers that were left lying on the bench and stowed them away into her bag before Jay could examine them more closely. Was now the right time to break the news about her identity? She decided against it, in view of their uncertain future.

'You've dropped your driving licence,' he remarked.

'Thanks.' Had he seen her name? She hoped not as she didn't want him to find her out this way.

'If there's nothing I can do, I might go back across to work. There are a few things I still need to do. Will you be all right?'

'Of course I will. I might wander down to the café after all. The police have my mobile number if they want to contact me. I'll see you later.'

She went down the hill, slowly. Her parents would be sure to come down to Cornwall and do their best to seek her out. She remembered the man who'd recognised her when she was working on reception. He'd be sure to comment that he'd seen her. The mess she had created was compounding by the minute.

*   *   *

The café was busy and Audrey was looking quite flustered.

'Do you want some help?' Georgie asked.

'Oh, bless you dear. Don't know where they're all coming from this morning.'

'It's turned quite chilly out there. Think people are wanting to get out of the wind. I'll just grab my apron and make a start.'

At least being busy took her mind off her troubles. It was well after lunchtime that Audrey was able to ask for news of the car.

'There isn't any news. They think it might have been stolen to order. They put new numbers plates on and re-spray the cars. Isn't that awful?'

'Indeed it is. Make us a pot of tea, will you love? And help yourself to something to eat. You're looking a bit pale. I suppose it's the shock of it all. What a dreadful business,' she said.

If only Audrey knew just how much of a shock she was suffering. It seemed an age since this morning when she had first suspected she could be pregnant.

The afternoon was less busy and they cleared up in plenty of time before closing. Her phone had remained stubbornly silent all afternoon. There was nothing she could do. When she got back to the caravan, Jay had tidied up and had even set the table for dinner. He'd put out two candles and a small vase of flowers, probably from the dining room, she thought, but it was a lovely gesture.

'What's all this'?' she asked.

'I thought you deserved a bit of a treat after

all the shocks of the morning. I've ordered dinner from the restaurant and there's champagne in the fridge. Go and have a shower and change and I'll be waiting for you.'

'Oh Jay. The table looks lovely. Thank you. But aren't you working this evening?'

'No. I've swapped duties till tomorrow.'

She did as she was told and she changed into one of her better outfits, wanting to make the effort for him.

'You look lovely,' he said softly, drawing her close to him. 'That's the blouse you wore when we first went out together. Makes your eyes look very blue.'

'Used to match my car too,' she said sadly before she could stop herself.

'Come on now love. This is supposed to make you forget about your woes. I'll open the champagne.' Expertly, he popped the cork and poured them a glass each. 'I borrowed the glasses too,' he laughed.

'Sorry I was so mopey. Thank you for doing all of this.' She was halfway down the glass when she remembered that she might be pregnant. You weren't supposed to drink, were you? She said nothing and continued to drink. One glass wouldn't do any harm and it could be a false alarm anyway.

'I'll go and collect our meal now. You sit there and try to relax. Won't be long.'

How sweet, she thought. He may not be taking her out for expensive meals at fancy restaurants but this was even better. The hotel's chef had a good reputation and she could look forward to something delicious.

It was a lovely evening, gentle, romantic and exactly what she needed to make up for the terrible day. It was almost ten o'clock when her phone rang.

'Hello you,' Jenny said.

'Hi Jenny.'

'Just wondered if you've any news for me.'

'Not really. Except that someone's stolen my car.'

'Not your lovely Blue Peril?'

'Indeed. Don't know who or when but the police are taking care of it.'

'And your other dilemma?'

'No progress as yet.'

'I take it you can't talk?'

'That's right. Jay's just poured champagne into me and provided a delicious meal so I mustn't be long.'

'Well, that sounds like progress.'

'I guess so. I'll call you when there's any news.'

'Make sure you do. And take great care. Hope the champers isn't a problem.'

'Course not. Night love.'

'What did the lovely Jenny want?' Jay asked.

'Just seeing how I am and how things are going. Shocked to hear about the car.'

'Maybe it could be a blessing in disguise. If you get the insurance money for it, we could

. . . sorry, you could buy something more practical to drive and still have cash left over. Clear your debts and make life easier for you.'

'For us, you really mean. I won't get anything for ages. I might get the loan of a car until there's some news but don't start counting your chickens. It could take weeks.'

'Of course it could. Sorry, I was thinking too far ahead. We do need to make plans. Everything here comes to an end in two or three weeks.'

'I thought you were planning to rent a bedsit near your college or something.'

'I wasn't really thinking straight. We can hardly live in a bedsit, can we?'

'Oh, so I'm included in your plans, am I?'

'Well, yes. Of course you are.' He looked a little surprised for a moment but smiled his glorious smile which completely melted her heart. 'Shall we go to bed now?' He reached for her and touched her cheek. His gentle fingers explored her face and touched her lips sending waves of desire through her. It was all going to be all right. This might even be a good time to confess the truth.

CHAPTER NINE

The feeling of sickness persisted the next morning and Georgie was now convinced that she must be pregnant. She hadn't slept well and had lain still for much of the night, not wanting to disturb Jay or let him see she was worried. It had been a long night.

Fortunately, Jay had left the caravan early so she was able to get up slowly and deal with the waves of nausea that were assailing her body.

She hated being sick at the best of times and this certainly wasn't one of the best. She absolutely must get a pregnancy test as soon as possible.

The opportunity to talk simply hadn't happened the previous evening. Jay fell asleep almost immediately. Should she say anything about the baby or wait till the confessions were out of the way first?

The police rang to report their progress, or lack of it.

'I'm sorry to say Madame, but we have found no trace of your stolen car. We've got alerts out nationwide and the local ports are also on the lookout. We'll keep you posted over the coming days.'

'Thank you. It's very upsetting to think this can happen in such a quiet village.'

'Way of life these days, I'm afraid. Did you get any joy from the insurance?'

'Not yet, I'm afraid. Thanks for your efforts, though.'

* * *

119

'You still look a bit pale,' Audrey told her when she arrived at the café. 'Are you all right?'

'Just worried about my car I suppose. I didn't sleep well.'

'If you want me to call Wendy in, I can do. You look as if you need a rest.'

'I'm fine. Besides, I need the money if I'm honest. They say two can live as cheaply as one but it doesn't seem to work out that way.'

It was late afternoon, as she was finishing work, she saw the large car driving up the hill towards the hotel. She recognised the model and colour. She watched as a man and woman went into reception. Her parents had arrived.

'Oh heavens, no,' she muttered.

'What is it dear?' Audrey asked. 'I'm getting quite concerned about you. You look as if you've seen a ghost.'

'I have, in a way. Someone I know has just driven up to the Clarence. Look, do you think I could leave in a minute? The rush is over but it means I shall be leaving you with extra clearing up to do.'

'You get off dear. I'll finish up now. It's almost closing time anyway,' she said taking a tray of mugs from Georgie.

'Thank you so much. Sorry, Audrey. I'll make up the time another day.'

'Don't worry about it. You do your fair share of the work every day. You go. And I hope it's good news.'

She dashed off and almost ran up the hill, desperate to get there before her cover was totally blown. She was praying that Jay hadn't met them and that they hadn't told him who she was. She was panting with the effort and cursing herself that she hadn't followed her instincts and told him the truth last night.

She rushed into reception, unaware that she still wore the silly cap and her Beach Café T-shirt. Her mother was sitting at one of the tables in the reception area, while her father was making his presence felt at the desk.

'I know my daughter is here, working at your reception desk. I don't know what she's told you but I have a friend who visited and saw her.'

'I assure you sir, we have no one by the name of Georgina Hetherington working here.'

'Don't try lying to me young woman. If she's told you not to reveal her name, then just realise who I am. My name carries great weight in the hotel world.'

'Yes sir, I certainly recognise the name. It isn't a common surname so of course I'd have known if your daughter was working here.'

'Don't you take up references?'

'Of course we do sir. Nobody working here can do so without proper references.'

Mrs Hetherington joined her husband.

'Don't make a fuss dear. It's obvious this

121

young lady doesn't know Georgina.'

The girl looked startled.

'Actually, we do have a Gina working for us part time. She does occasional cover when someone's off sick.' She saw Georgie rush in through the doors. 'Oh, here she is right now.'

'Georgie, darling,' her mother said, rushing over to her. She enveloped her in a hug, much to her daughter's embarrassment.

'Mummy. Daddy. I asked you not to come. How did you know where I was?'

'Someone Daddy knows visited here one evening and recognised you. He mentioned it to your father when we arrived in Cornwall yesterday.'

'What the hell are you wearing?' her father demanded.

'Sorry. I came straight from work when I saw your car.'

'But I thought you worked here?' Mrs Hetherington said.

'I do I suppose, but only occasionally. Mostly I work at a café in the village.'

'Good grief. My daughter, a waitress.' Her father sighed.

Georgie tried to draw them away from the receptionist who was staring wide eyed at the spectacle. It would certainly provide a good story for later.

'Nothing wrong with being a waitress,' Georgie told them.

'But please, can we move to somewhere a

little more private?'

'Where are you living?' her father asked.

'Well, I'm . . . I'm sharing a caravan. We can sit out on the terrace, if you like.'

'This gets better and better. You're sharing a caravan. My daughter living in a caravan.' The emphasis he placed on the words made it sound like the worst kind of slum imaginable.

'Waitresses are poorly paid and the apartment I was renting became too expensive. If you remember, you cancelled payment of my credit card.'

'Oh darling, but you said you could manage,' her mother gasped. 'I can't believe you were short of money.'

'You can't seriously think I'd go on supporting you when you were behaving so badly.' Her father's face was a furious red.

'I've managed. It just meant compromising.'

'And what's happened to your car?'

'It was stolen. The police have no trace yet.'

'You are possibly the most irresponsible person I know. How could you be so careless?'

'I can hardly control the entire population of robbers and criminals. It's everywhere Daddy. There's a crime wave in case you hadn't noticed.'

'If it had been left safely locked in the garage at home, it wouldn't have been stolen.'

'With whom are you sharing?' her mother asked, trying desperately to move the conversation away from recriminations.

Georgie blushed furiously. She opened her mouth to speak and saw Jay going into the dining room. He paused and came towards her. He put a hand on her shoulder.

'Is everything all right?'

'Jay, I should introduce you to my mother and father. This is Jay Jacobs. I'm sharing with him. Jay, my parents.' He stared for a moment. Her mother extended a polite hand.

'Fay Hetherington,' she said graciously. 'Do I take it you're more than . . . what's the correct term? Room mates?'

'Well, yes. Mrs Hetherington. Mr Hetherington.' He seemed to have taken the name change rather well, Georgie thought nervously clutching at Jay's hand. 'And I want you to know that I love and respect your daughter,' he said, squeezing Georgie's hand protectively.

'I'll bet you do,' snapped her father. 'Waiter are you? That's a waiter's uniform you're wearing.'

'Jay's studying hotel management. He's been working for the summer before he returns to college.'

'And you saw my daughter as an easy way into a decent job I suppose?'

'Nothing of the sort, sir.'

'I'll bet. Not too many Hetheringtons around, are there? I expect you saw the name and made your move.'

Jay went white with anger. Georgie clutched

his hand tightly, trying to stop him from saying anything they might all regret. Her father had a temper that brooked no argument. If they were ever to make a future of any sort, Jay mustn't get into one of the terrible sorts of row she had heard his employees subjected to in the past.

'If you must know, Jay had no idea of my real name. He doesn't know who I am. Strange as it may seem to you, he fell in love with Gina Hind. A simple waitress at the Beach Café.'

'You've lost your mind girl. He didn't bat an eyelid when he heard our name. If you think you got away with some sort of pseudonym, you were living in a dream. Of course he knew who you were, you silly child.'

Georgie grimaced, remembering exactly why she had left home in the first place.

'I have known since yesterday, as it happens.' Jay spoke calmly and quietly. 'When Georgie's car was stolen, I saw her name on her driving licence and insurance documents. I couldn't resist looking up the name. I've only called her Gina and not Georgie, at least since her friend came to visit.'

'You mean to say, Jenny's been to see you?'

'Well, yes. She came for a weekend.'

'That naughty girl. I've been asking her to give me a clue as to your whereabouts,' her father said, shaking his head.

'I swore her to secrecy. I didn't want you charging down and trying to take over my life yet again. Just like you're doing now.'

'But you're coming back with us, aren't you darling?' Mrs Hetherington pleaded, reaching out to touch her daughter's arm.

'I don't think so Mummy. Not yet. Jay and I have a lot of things to settle and talk about.' She looked up at him, her eyes begging him to say something to agree with her.

'If you really believe he didn't know who you were right from the start, you must be an idiot. How do you explain a sports car that cost in excess of thirty thousand pounds?' her father blustered, his face crimson.

'I said I'd won in it in a competition.'

'You devious little madam! I'm washing my hands of you. Come along Fay. I no longer have a daughter!'

'Please sir. Hear us out. Let me organise some tea and biscuits and we can talk.' Jay let go of Georgie's hand and seemed to be taking command of the situation. 'Please. It isn't what you think at all.'

'I'd love some tea. Thank you, Jay. Please darling, let's give them a chance to explain.' Mrs Hetherington caught at her husband's arm and held him back. The scowl never left his face but he relented and allowed himself to be led towards a table.

Georgie gave a weak smile of gratitude to her mother. Mrs Hetherington usually managed to get what she wanted.

Jay came to join them and one of the

126

waitresses arrived a few minutes later with a tray of tea and cakes. Georgie leaned forward to pour and handed a cup to her mother. Jay passed the cakes and smiled.

'Thank you for giving us the chance to talk. I'd like to explain. I certainly had no idea at all that Georgie was anyone other than who she said she was. A waitress, Gina Hind, working here for the summer and with no great ideas of what she wanted to do. Of course I realised she had a good education and was probably wasted doing the job she was. When I saw her name on the driving licence yesterday, I recognised the name of course. Anyone working in hospitality knows the name and reputation of Hetherington Hotels.'

'Why didn't you say something?' Georgie asked him.

'I was waiting for you to tell me yourself, and anyway, I didn't want to spoil our evening.'

She smiled but had a momentary doubt flit through her brain. Last night's meal had been very special and he'd produced champagne. Why had he chosen that particular time to do it? Precisely when he had discovered her true identity? Odd timing, when he had been complaining about his cash shortage days earlier. She smiled and made no comment.

'So, how long have you been seeing each other?' Mrs Hetherington asked.

'A few weeks.'

'It took me a while to pluck up courage to

ask her out,' Jay confessed. 'I didn't think I stood a chance but I was lucky and well, we fell in love.'

'Yes well, that's as maybe, but the situation has changed now. She'll be coming back with us to take up her rightful place in the business. You'd better pack your things, Georgina. We shall be leaving in the morning. I have a few things to sort out at the Hetherington this evening. I'll come and collect you at nine o'clock sharp tomorrow.'

'No Daddy. I'm not going back with you. Jay and I are together. I'll tell you when—and if—I'm coming back.'

'What's got into you. If you don't come now, then I shall disown you. Nothing more to do with you. Clear enough? We'll see if this waiter still wants you then.'

Jay was listening, his face white and eyes flashing in anger. He said nothing but the tight line of his lips proved how hard he was fighting his temper.

'I'm sorry Mummy, Daddy, but I can't just leave in this way. Jay and I . . . well, we need to talk. There are things I want to tell him and we need to discuss the future. Besides, I do have a job, I can't let the owner down, whatever you think about me being irresponsible.'

'You call that a job?' her father sniffed. 'Very well. This is your last chance, Georgina. You can phone me if you want to be collected. Otherwise, you're on your own.' Mr

Hetherington stood up, dropping crumbs from his cake all over the carpet. He flung down his napkin, knocking over one of the cups. 'Come along Fay.'

He turned and stormed out of the hotel. Her mother hesitated and gave her daughter a quick hug.

'I'm sorry but I'll have to go with him. He'll calm down eventually. Leave him to me. I'll be in touch soon. Do take care darling. Goodbye, Jay. Look after her, won't you?'

'Of course I will. Nice to meet you at last.'

'Keep in touch, darling. Don't leave us worrying . . . please.'

'All right, Mummy. I'll let you know our plans when we've made them.' She walked to the door with her mother and Jay stayed behind, clearing up the mess that had been left.

'I can quite see why you like him, dear. He's rather gorgeous, isn't he? But you will be careful, won't you? Be certain before you commit yourself to anything. And I'll try to organise something regarding a car. You can't be left without transport. I'll get Daddy's secretary to sort things out with the insurance.'

'Thank you, Mummy. And . . . well . . . I'm sorry to give you so much worry, but you see how Daddy is. Trying to organise my life. At least I know for sure that Jay loves me for myself and not who I am.'

There was a loud honking of a car horn.

'Sorry, I must go. See you soon.'

She got into the car and turned to wave. Her father drove away throwing up a spray of gravel behind him. She went back inside to Jay. He looked up, an expression on his face that she couldn't fathom.

'We need to talk,' he said simply. 'I'll have to work this evening but I'll try to get away early.'

'Okay. I'm sorry you had to face that without warning.'

'Not to worry. It had to happen sometime. I'll see you later.' He carried the tray into the kitchen, leaving her alone.

Slowly, she went across to the caravan, her mind racing in all directions. She had to admit to missing her family, despite her father's ways. She was used to dealing with him but sometimes it was too much to cope with.

Her mother was so gentle by comparison but usually managed to get her own way when she needed to.

Georgie smiled as she thought of her mother's comments about Jay. But she knew she had to be cautious about what she said to him. He had produced an expensive meal just on the very day he had discovered her true identity. Coincidence? Maybe but she doubted it. It did give her a bit of a jolt. He was not beyond a bit of deviousness but she could hardly blame him under the circumstances. Nevertheless, it made her suspicious of what might happen next. She also needed to get this pregnancy testing kit but without a car, she could hardly go and buy one in the nearest town. Should she risk getting one at the chemist in the village? People might talk if she did. But then, she needed to know before their talk got much further. She glanced at her watch. They'd be closing in ten minutes but if she hurried, she might just get there in time. She grabbed her purse and almost ran down the hill.

'Hi Gina,' the chemist's assistant greeted her. 'Just in time. Can I help?' Georgie couldn't do it.

'Just need some paracetamol,' she lied.

She would have to get into town somehow and buy her kit somewhere more anonymous. She couldn't say anything about being pregnant to Jay until she knew for sure. Whatever the future held, they had to find a way to earn money to live on. Oh, how would she spend the next few hours until Jay finished work?

What a mess!

CHAPTER TEN

Georgie had sat in front of the tiny television for an hour but had no idea what she'd watched. She made some toast. If she really was pregnant, she needed to eat something more nutritious. She nibbled at a piece of cheese and ate a tomato, but everything was too much hassle and she still faced a difficult talk with Jay.

She heard him crunching across the gravel at nine-thirty and opened the door for him. She held out her hands to him, expecting him to take them and pull her close. He ignored the gesture and almost pushed past her.

'Jay?' she whispered. He sat on the sofa and patted the seat for her to sit beside him. She frowned. She had expected him to try and comfort her after the trauma of meeting her parents, for him to be sympathetic and not this distant, remote shell.

'We have to be realistic Georgie. We have totally different backgrounds. If I'd realised who you were, we would never have become close the way we have. I can never expect to give you the sort of life you're used to. You need to call your parents and go back to your life with them.'

'What are you saying, Jay? You don't love me after all?'

'It doesn't matter what I think or feel. You have a good life. You have everything you could want provided for you. I'm offering a bedsit somewhere and a very uncertain future.'

'But Jay, you must realise that I'd choose you over any luxuries and wealth. Why do you think I left it all behind in the first place?

You've seen what my father's like. He wants his own way all the time and doesn't listen to anyone else's ideas or care what makes them happy. He thinks that I live a happy life if I have a decent car and a few pieces of jewellery. I used to spend my time shopping and meeting friends for lunches. The times I worked in the hotels were all good but then, he considered it little more than occupational therapy for me.'

'But you could do it. I saw the way you worked the reception here. You managed it far better than most of the permanent staff. In fact, I know the manager was going to offer you a permanent job here. He asked me what your plans were and I said we were probably moving on. Sorry, I should have asked you, I suppose. You'll accuse me of trying to organise your life.'

'Maybe, but I wouldn't have taken it anyway, not unless you were staying.'

'I can see exactly why you kept your identity a secret. It must have been difficult for you to form relationships with men.'

'Of course it was. Anyone who came near, Daddy sent them packing, assuming they were only after my money. Says something about the sort of man he is, doesn't it?'

'He wants the best for you. And I'm not it.'

'But you are the best for me, Jay. I love you. I thought you loved me, too.'

'I do, but I simply can't take everything away from you. You'd resent it one day. If we were living in a bedsit with no money and pathetic jobs, you'd grow to hate me. We find it hard enough to live in this caravan at times. I bet you have your own bathroom at home that's larger than this entire caravan.' He sighed.

'So what if it is? I've lived for several months like this and not minded at all.'

'But this has been a sort of holiday for you. A breakout from the normal life you live. You could go back any time.'

'So, what are you saying? You don't care any more and you want me to leave?'

'I think it would be for the best. You have until early tomorrow to call your parents.'

She tried to read his expression but his face was like some sort of mask. He was hiding his emotions from her and she didn't know whether to believe him.

'I love you Jay. Do you want to throw it all away in some strange belief that it's a transient whim?'

'Oh Georgie, don't make it so difficult for me. I'm trying to do what's best for both of us.'

'What you think may be best. You're as bad as my father.' A flicker of pain ran over his face. 'Do you want me to move out now or can we have one more night together?'

'Of course I don't want you to move out. Come here.' He drew her close and she felt him trembling. She stroked his forehead and ran her fingers into his dark hair. He kissed her and she felt her emotions surge in the

134

wonderful way she had become used to over the past weeks.

'Come on. Let's go to bed,' she whispered.

It was going to be all right. He still loved her. As she lay in his arms, she felt deep contentment wash over her. He had slipped into a deep sleep and she lay still, not wanting to move and break the spell he had woven around her.

She felt his even breathing and gently touched his chest. Fine black hairs felt silky smooth beneath her fingers. She could no longer imagine a night without him sleeping beside her and she gave an involuntary shudder at the thought of leaving him. Eventually, she fell into a light sleep and dreamt of sunny days and sea. She awoke to hear rain drumming down on the roof. She gave a jolt which woke Jay.

'What's the matter?' he murmured.

'Nothing. I just woke suddenly as the rain was falling so hard. Sorry. Go back to sleep. I didn't mean to wake you,' she said.

'What's the time?'

'Dunno. It's still dark so it must be early.' Jay disengaged himself from her arms and turned to look at his watch.

'Six o'clock. Shouldn't you start packing?'

'But why? I'm not going anywhere. I thought . . . Well, after last night . . . I thought you didn't want me to go.'

'I thought we'd discussed it all. I want what

135

is best for you.'

'You don't. It's what you think is best, but you're wrong. I'm not going anywhere. If you don't want to be with me any more, then I'll find somewhere else to live. Audrey offered me a room while I look.'

'You're as stubborn as your father, you realise.'

'Possibly.'

'Of course I don't want to lose you, Georgie. I love you. I do want to be with you but I'm . . . well, I have very little money and no prospects.'

'We'll do something together to make our own fortunes, you wait and see. If my father can start with nothing and end up with a hotel empire, why shouldn't we?'

'But you heard what he said. If you don't call him now, that's it. You'll lose everything—forever.'

'Maybe. My mother said she would organise the car insurance claim. We should get a decent sum in compensation. I can buy a cheaper car and we'll have a decent start towards our living expenses.'

'I won't live off you. It's no way to make our future.'

'Forget your stupid pride! I want us to be together and if that's the way to make it happen, then so be it. We might even have the deposit for a flat to rent. And I can get a job anyway. As you say, I have lots of talents to support us while you get your qualifications.'

He looked unhappy again and was about to say something but changed his mind.

'I'll have to get up. I need a shower and it will be time to serve the wretched breakfasts again soon. Never ending, isn't it?' He left her and she snuggled into his warm place. She heard the water running and hugged her arms round herself. Everything was going to be all right. Except for one thing. If she was going to have a baby, she wouldn't be able to work and well, babies cost a lot of money, didn't they? Still, once her parents became grandparents, they would surely forgive everything and help them out. Jay might not like the idea but he'd have no choice in the matter. She sat up and immediately felt the waves of nausea beginning. Jay came back to the bedroom, a towel hung round his middle.

'Mmm, you look tempting. If I didn't have to serve breakfast to dozens of guests, I'd creep back in there with you.' He paused. 'Are you all right? You look pale.'

'Tension, I expect. It's been a difficult few days. You'd better get dressed and get to work or someone will come knocking at the door for you. I'd better get moving too. Audrey has no idea what's going on. I left work early yesterday.'

As soon as she was sure Jay had gone, she rushed to the toilet and was sick. If nothing else was to convince her, that was a clear sign of pregnancy. She hadn't realised morning sickness could start so early and wondered how long it lasted. She washed herself and held a cool flannel on her forehead. This was awful. Even so, she still needed to do a proper test to be certain before she told Jay.

Audrey gave her a perfect opportunity when she arrived at work a little later.

'I was wondering if you could do me a big favour?' she asked.

'Surely, if I can.'

'My husband's been called away. His mother's ill.'

'Oh dear. I'm sorry.'

'Nothing serious but she does flap a bit. It means he hasn't done the cash and carry run. I was wondering if you'd mind going for me? We have the van. It's a bit ancient but it goes all right.'

'Of course I will. I'd be pleased to help. Or shall I mind this place if you want to go yourself?'

'Oh no, dear. I don't actually like driving. I have a licence but I don't drive if I can help it. If you can go right away, you'll be back for the main coffee time. It's not far and I've made out a list.'

Georgie drove away from the village. The van was indeed elderly and had very little power. It was probably something she would have to get used to, driving an older, rickety car.

She passed a chemist in the town and stopped outside. She ran in and collected a pregnancy testing kit, frowning slightly at the cost but at least she now had it and could confirm things one way or the other. She stuffed it into her handbag and got back into the van.

It was an interesting trip to the wholesale store. On her way back, she stopped in a layby to read the test instructions. It was going to have to wait until she finished work and then she hoped Jay would be working long enough for her to do it privately.

It seemed a long day and she grew more and more tense as the time approached. Jenny rang her during the afternoon, hoping for an update.

'I gather you've had an official visitation,' she said.

'I guess Mummy has called you?'

'Oh yes. I was told off for not letting them know you were all right. Anyway, what's the news?'

'I've only just managed to buy a test kit. I'll do it after work. Did Mummy say anything about Jay?'

'Only that she could see why you were smitten. She admitted he left Guy way behind in some ways and she found Jay quite charming. Sorry, have to go love. I've just grabbed a minute between clients. Good luck. Speak soon.'

'Yes. I'd like a chat. Bye.'

Later that evening and shaking slightly she sat staring at the little strip. The line changed colour. Positive. She shivered, partly with excitement and partly with fear. She screwed up the box and threw it in the bin. The sensor itself, she left in her toilet bag, planning to show it to Jay later. This all confirmed one thing. She had made the right decision not to go back with her parents. She and Jay would get married and have their family. She felt nervous and excited all rolled into one. She wondered how she should break the news. Should she just come out with it? Wait until they were both relaxed? Cook a special meal?

He came in briefly between his afternoon and evening shifts.

'Sorry love but I'm having to make up for the time I took off and there's some overtime on offer. I need to take it. We have a lot to talk about so I'll see you later.'

'Fine. Yes, there's heaps to talk about,' she agreed.

Would this tension ever come to an end? Always there seemed to be something new. Another long evening loomed ahead. Maybe she should go for a walk but it wasn't warm and looked as if it might rain again. Her phone rang. Her mother.

'Hello, Mummy,' she replied.

'How are you?'

'I'm all right. Just waiting for Jay to

finish. How are things with you? Daddy less explosive?'

'I wouldn't say that. Bear with a sore head comes to mind. He's missing you terribly but he won't admit it. I just wanted to tell you, I've spoken to Daddy's PA. She says the insurers won't pay up until the police search is finally concluded.'

'That's just great. What am I supposed to do in the meantime?' she exclaimed.

'Well, they will pay for a courtesy car for two weeks and then review it. Have you spoken to the police again?'

'No, but they said they would contact me if there was any news. Still, if I can have something for a week or two, that's good. What do I have to do?'

Her mother gave her the information and then hesitated.

'You are certain you won't come back? We do miss you and whatever he said at the time, Daddy isn't going to turn you away if you return.'

'I'm not planning on coming back, I'm afraid. Except maybe to visit if I'm welcome.'

'I see. Well, it's your decision. I'm sorry you feel that way but I can understand—but if you ever change your mind you know we'll be here for you. I do like your Jay. He's terribly good looking but I hope for your sake there's more to him than a handsome face.'

'Oh, I think so. He has ambition and he's

intelligent. What more could I want?'

'Someone capable of earning a decent living. Do you think you'll marry him?'

'We haven't talked about it but I hope so.'

'Keep in touch, won't you? We worry about you so much.'

'Of course, Mummy.'

'And please let me know if you're short of money. I don't want you making do again. I've got money of my own so Daddy need never know.'

'Thank you. I'll remember, but I suspect Jay is far too independent to accept help.'

'Independence is only affordable as long as you're not starving. Goodbye now. I love you darling.'

Georgie wondered later how her mother would feel about becoming a grandparent. Probably shocked. She would certainly expect them to be married before the baby was born. Marriage. What a huge decision but she really had no doubts that it was what she wanted more than anything, as long as Jay Jacobs was the bridegroom.

*   *   *

When Jay came back he was totally exhausted. He flopped down on the sofa and almost fell asleep immediately. She made him a hot drink and gave it to him.

'Thanks. Look, I know there's a lot we want

to discuss but I am totally shattered. Can we leave it till tomorrow? I'll have some time off then but it's been a ridiculous day. I have the evening off tomorrow. We can do something if you like.'

'Let's wait and see how it goes. What time are you going on duty tomorrow?'

'Around the middle of the day,' he murmured, not specifying exactly when.

'You could always come to the café for some coffee.'

'I'm not sure. Maybe. Let's go to bed. I feel as if I could sleep for days.'

'All right. If that's what you want.'

She lay awake beside him. He'd fallen asleep as soon as he lay down. She cuddled close to his back but he seemed unaware of her. Her mind was still turning over and over and sleep was far away. How was he going to take the news? He must surely be pleased, even though their future was still somewhat uncertain. Tomorrow, it had to be.

For whatever reason, when she awoke the sickness seemed less intense. It was fortunate as Jay lay in bed, watching her get ready for work.

'You're very beautiful,' he murmured lazily. 'It's such a pity you have to be at work this morning.'

'Well, we can't all be idle slobs. What are you going to do with your morning off?'

'Haven't decided. I might do something

exciting like the washing or go shopping.'

'Proper housewife, aren't you?'

'Watch it you. Get yourself off to work.'

'I forgot to say. The insurers say I can have a hire car for a couple of weeks. I'll call the garage and see what's available.'

'Great. That will be good—if we ever have time to use it! Still, make a change from going everywhere by bus.'

She looked at him quizzically.

'Where do you go on the bus?' she asked innocently.

'Into town usually. Shopping and stuff,' he hedged. 'Aren't you going to be late?'

'Yes. I'll go. See you this evening. We must have that talk.' She reached over and kissed the top of his head. He smiled and blew her a kiss.

* * *

When she was having her morning break, she saw Jay rushing down the hill and leaping onto the bus as it was leaving. Odd, she thought. He'd said he was working the lunchtime shift. She gave a shrug. Obviously something had come up. She thought no more about it but he was not home when she arrived back. She began to prepare something for supper and left it ready to finish off when he returned.

She went across to the hotel to see if he was there at eight o'clock. Nobody had seen him all day and the implication was that he had had the day off. Why had he said he was working, in that case?

She saw another service bus coming in and was relieved to see him getting off it. She went down the hill to meet him.

'Hello you. Where've you been all day?'

'Had some business to sort out. Sorry I wasn't back. Hope you didn't wait to eat.'

'Course I did. I've cooked supper and it's waiting to be heated through.'

'I'm sorry. I got something in town.'

'You might have called or texted. I wouldn't have bothered going to all that effort just for myself.'

'Sorry, I didn't think. Do you want to go to the pub and have something there? I think there's a band on tonight.'

'We still need to talk, Jay. I have something to tell you. It's important . . .' she said.

They arrived at the caravan and he looked at the little table, carefully laid and with a candle ready to light.

'I'm so sorry. I'd no idea you'd go to any trouble.'

She shrugged trying not to let her irritation show. *Where could he have been for so long?* she wondered.

'What's so important then?'

'Only our whole future together. I assume you do want us to have a future?'

'Of course I do. But it's too soon to discuss

it in detail. I think you need to make things up with your parents first and foremost. Whatever they said at the time, I can't believe they'd reject their only daughter.'

'And if I don't?'

'As I said before, you'll regret it.'

'Actually, there's something you should hear first.'

He stared at her and frowned, worried by her tone.

'I'm pregnant. You're going to be a father.'

'What?' he almost yelled. 'You can't be! You can't possibly be having a baby. I don't believe it! No, no, no!' He got up and stomped around the tiny room. 'No Gina. Georgie. No. You're not having my baby. Damn it! No!'

'That went well,' Georgie muttered. 'Look, I'm sorry Jay but it's true. I am pregnant. I did a test yesterday and it was positive. Is positive. I'll show you if you don't believe me.'

'These tests are never certain. Oh, no. Not again! I don't believe it. Weren't you taking precautions?'

'Well, not to start with. You knew how inexperienced I was . . .'

Her voice was shaky and feeble with the shock of his reaction.

'But you wanted it. You invited me into your home. Naturally I assumed you knew what you were doing. How could you? I can't have children, I can't!' He went outside, slamming the door behind him, indicating she shouldn't follow him.

Her tears fell unchecked. Why on earth was he so angry with her? If he was so worried about it, he should have used contraceptives. Admittedly, she had given little or no thought to it at the beginning.

This was the very last reaction she had been expecting. She'd thought he'd be pleased. What had he said before she broke the news? Make up with your parents? He had treated her to a meal and champagne the very day he had learned who she was. How could she have been so stupid? He was just like the rest of the boyfriends she'd had. He wanted her for her connections and wealth. Her father was right all along. She should only ever consider marrying someone like Guy. He was an equal. But Guy? Sweet man though he was, she did not love him. She closed her eyes and could only see Jay's handsome face and lithe body. There was nobody else she had ever met who came anywhere near to him. He had filled her life and her mind since they first met.

Sobs wracked her body. Her eyes were swollen and she felt sick once more. She rushed to the toilet and splashed cold water on her face and sat down again. Jay's reaction had been extreme and what had he said about not being able to have children? It was ridiculous. She had never been near anyone else and he knew that. Round and round her mind went. What had he said? Not again? What on earth did he mean by that?

She stood outside the caravan and looked for him. Perhaps he'd gone to the pub to get a drink. She could have done with something herself and considered going to the hotel bar to get a brandy but, in her current state, that wasn't a good idea. There was no sign of Jay so she turned and came back inside.

She lay on the sofa, not wanting to go to bed in case he came back. By midnight, it was clear he wasn't going to return.

The next morning she felt awful. Little sleep and the upset had done their worst. She phoned Audrey.

'Are you all right dear? Do you need anything?' she asked.

'I'll be fine. Sorry to let you down.'

'Don't worry. I think the season is about over so I'll be able to manage. Have you had any more thoughts on my offer of a permanent job, or are you returning home?'

'I'm afraid not. You're right, I should think about going back to Hertfordshire.'

'And what about your young man? Is he well or has he got the same bug as you?'

'Oh . . . he's all right.' She found herself near to tears again and clenched her fist, determined not to break down again.

'Well get better soon and don't hurry back until you're quite well. I must say, you've looked a bit peaky for the last few days. You're sure there's nothing serious wrong?'

148

'I'll be fine. Thanks. See you soon.' She switched off her phone and slumped down on the sofa. What on earth was she going to do? Where could Jay have gone? She showered and tried to make herself look a little more respectable. She decided to see if he was in the hotel or another caravan on the site. They couldn't possibly leave things like this. There was a knock at the door. It was the duty manager.

'Is Jay here? He hasn't turned up for his shift' He was clearly irritated and snapped out the words.

'He's not here, I'm afraid.'

'So where is he? It's not good enough. He called in sick yesterday and now he's failed to arrive for work and not even notified me.'

Georgie felt tears pressing again and managed to stammer, 'He went out last night and hasn't come back all night. I'm very worried about him.'

The manager softened a little.

'I know he's been having time off to sort a few problems lately but I can't let it affect his work. He's become quite unreliable and this just doesn't work in our business.'

Georgie stared. What were these problems? He hadn't mentioned anything to her and as far as she knew, he had been at work as usual. Except for yesterday, of course.

'Did he say in what connection the problems were?'

'Some family business. But you're a couple, aren't you? I'm sorry. I assumed you'd know.' He watched as the girl seemed to crumble in front of him. 'I'm sorry,' he repeated. 'I hope I haven't breached a confidence.'

'No, no. It's all right. I'm just a bit upset. We had a row last night and then he didn't come home and . . .' She broke off, unable to say anything more without breaking down completely.

'Well, if he does contact you, let him know he's on a final warning. I can't continue to employ someone who is unreliable.'

'He'll be leaving soon anyway, won't he? When the college term starts again.'

'What college? First I've heard of it.'

'But I thought he was only here temporarily. For the summer.'

'It seems you need to talk to him. He's been working here for well over a year now. I'm sorry. I must get back. I have to find someone to cover his lunchtime shift as well.'

'Of course. Bye.' She shut the door and sat down again. The shock of even more of his lies was too much to handle. What were the family problems the manager referred to? As far as she knew the family he had were in Devon. He could hardly have been going to Devon by the local bus, especially not in one day. There was too much she didn't know about the man she had believed was in love with her and whom she loved in return.

150

What should she do now?

CHAPTER ELEVEN

Georgie drifted around the caravan and hotel grounds for most of the morning. Each time the service bus came into the village, she started to walk down the hill to meet it. But there was no sign of Jay. She felt physically sick, not just morning sickness but with the pain of knowing she'd been lied to, that everything she had believed was based on nothing. She had allowed him into her life completely and trusted him like no one ever before. Perhaps she could understand why her parents had been protecting her so carefully. Should she call Jenny and share it with her? But what would she say? Jenny had warned her to take care. She would probably say it was her own fault for trusting him on so short an acquaintance. On the other hand, she was a good friend and would surely be sympathetic. She called Jenny's number.

'Georgie. What's the news?' At the sound of her friend's voice, she felt tears running down her face once more and her words were choked.

'Oh Jen, I'm in a terrible mess.'

'Georgie . . . What's happened? Are you all right?'

151

'No.'

'What's he done to you?'

'Made me pregnant and now he's run away.'

'What do you mean? Run away?'

'I told him and he was furious. Said terrible things like it couldn't be his. Said 'not again' and I don't know what that means,' she wailed.

'Oh Georgie. I take it you are definitely pregnant?'

'Yes. The test is positive and I'm still getting morning sickness. What am I going to do?'

'You could come home. Whatever they say, your parents would take you back, without a doubt.'

'I couldn't. I can't . . . Not like this. My father would be furious and never let me forget it.'

'There's the other solution of course.'

'What?'

'You don't have to keep it.'

'Don't be ridiculous. I couldn't. No, never. Whatever the problems, I couldn't possibly get rid of my baby. No, I'll have to find a way of coping on my own.'

'You'll never do it all alone. Don't be stupid. You've never had to manage alone in your life.'

'I know. But I have been managing recently.'

'Sort of. Have you got your car back?'

'No, but the insurance company will pay for a hire car for a while. If it isn't found, I'll get compensation and then I can buy something smaller and use the difference. That's what Jay and I had planned to do anyway.' Her voice choked again as she thought of their plans, now in ruins.

'Georgie, well . . . I don't suppose Jay had anything to do with the theft of your car?'

'Of course not. He was as shocked as I was when it went missing.' She stopped and thought about it. They had never found out when the spare set of keys had gone missing. Perhaps Jay had organised it with someone. There were a whole lot of things she didn't know about him.

'Is there anything else you know about him? Any clues to where he might be?'

'Not really. Oh, the manager came over to see why he wasn't at work this morning. He says Jay has worked here for months, not just the summer.'

'Look, why don't you bid farewell to Poltoon and come and stay with me for a few days. We can talk things through.'

'I couldn't. Suppose he comes back? There are so many things we need to sort out. Besides, I haven't got a car yet.'

'Well you need to sort that out for a start. How's Audrey with all of this?'

'I haven't told her anything. Just cancelled work today but she says the season's nearly over and she won't be needing me for much longer.'

'Then it sounds as if you're all clear.'

'But I have to earn money. At least until I decide what to do.'

'Have you any idea how much it costs to have a baby? I mean, to look after it properly. Provide stuff for it. Prams and cots and everything.'

'I can buy second-hand ones,' she replied bravely.

'Oh yes, of course. I can just see your parents allowing their grandchild to live in a second-hand pram. You're in shock right now. Don't do anything rash. Look around and see if there are any clues about where Jay might be hiding. Address book. Letters. Anything.'

'I couldn't. It's like spying.'

'For heaven's sakes, grow up Georgie! You're an adult with a baby growing inside you. Where's the sparky friend I used to have? The one intent on taking over the Hetherington Hotel chain one day?'

'She's somewhere lost in emotions she never knew existed.'

'I know. I'm sorry. I'll give you a day or two to get yourself organised with a car and a plan and if that hasn't happened, I'll come down and bounce you out of it all.'

'Thanks, Jen. I'm sorry to be so pathetic. You're right. I need to get things sorted. Promise you won't call my parents?'

'I'll promise for now, on condition you make proper plans.'

'I will. I feel better having talked it through.'

'Must go. My boss is glaring.'

Georgie made some coffee and started to look through some of the drawers. Jay had several drawers that he used for clothes and one for papers. Feeling terrible about doing it, she looked through his things. She picked up his bank statement and gritted her teeth to look at it. His wages were paid in monthly, as she would have expected. Not a great amount but with tips that weren't shown, it seemed reasonable and in line with what their own hotels would have paid to a waiter. He also had the caravan supplied as living accommodation so presumably that was deducted from his wage anyway.

There were regular payments made each month—just over a quarter of what he earned—but it didn't show where the payments were going. Perhaps it was money he was paying off for something? Or credit cards? But it was a regular sum and had been for several months.

She warmed her icy cold hands round her mug and braced herself to look for more information. There was a small book with some addresses in it and a few phone numbers but most of his contacts would be stored on his phone, as hers were.

Should she send him a text? It would have been easier than speaking to him but she still didn't want to be the one to make contact first. She found nothing to indicate where he might have gone. Maybe he had a friend in the village he could be staying with? But it was such a small place, she knew many of the people he knew. It was such a shock that he'd disappeared this way. If only she had met his sister or brother, she would have called them. Despite everything, she wanted to see his handsome face and those gorgeous green eyes looking down at her once more.

She put her hand on her stomach and wept tears of abject misery. Poor fatherless baby! What would be his or her future?

It was the longest day she could remember. Nobody heard from Jay. She went to speak to the manager who said that if Jay didn't return for his shift the next morning, he was fired with immediate effect.

'But what about the caravan? Does that mean I have to move out too?'

'Well, yes. I'm afraid so. You have until the end of next week but everything must be cleared out.'

'What do I do with all Jay's things, if he doesn't come back?'

'You'll have to store them in our trunk room if he doesn't return, but surely he will come back to collect everything. Look, I'm sorry if I was insensitive earlier. I can see you're upset and I suppose it means the end of a relationship for you. I don't want to rub it in but you're not his first lady friend. I suppose you must know that.'

'You mean someone else was living here before me?'

'I'm sorry, but yes.'

'Do you know who she was? Or where she lived?'

'It ended rather suddenly. Earlier this year. I believe she was a local girl. She worked in the kitchen here.'

'Does she live in the village?' Georgie demanded.

'In Redruth, I believe, but I'm not certain. Look, I shouldn't say any more. You need to sort things out between you. Did you ever hear any more about your missing car?'

'Nothing. I'll call the police again today and then I'm going to hire something.'

'You seem to have been very unlucky lately. Look, if it's of any help, I can offer you a more permanent position here. One of our receptionists is leaving soon. You're very good. I was impressed when you stood in. It would mean you could stay in the caravan for a while longer, if you wanted to. I don't recommend it in the winter, though you might get a long let in one of the holiday places then.'

'It's an idea,' she said gratefully. 'Thank you.' She left the office feeling a little more positive.

She telephoned the police but there was no further news of her missing car.

'I reckon they've got it hidden away somewhere, thinking the pressure will drop soon.'

'And will it?'

'Well, there's still a call out for the number and model. We'll be alerted if it's seen of course but they're sure to have changed the number plate by now. Might be worth looking at one of the online auction sites.'

'Thanks. I will. I'll get a hire car in the meantime.'

She switched off her phone and looked for the details her mother had given her. It was almost closing time for most garages but she called anyway to see if they had cars available. She gave her details and arranged to call in the next day. Then she called Audrey again and asked if she was needed in work the next morning.

'Not really, dear. I think maybe we can call it a day now for the season. If you call in when you're ready, you can collect your pay. I've enjoyed working with you Gina. You've been a wonderful help to me.'

'Seems as if everything's coming to an end,' she said sadly.

'Oh, we rather like getting our county back to ourselves again. The roads stop being quite so busy and life is much more peaceful. I'm lucky that my husband's in a permanent job. Means we can take things easier over the winter.'

'Thanks. I'll call in tomorrow when I get back.'

With a few more options in place, Georgie began to feel better. She was also hungry and looked to see what there was in the fridge. The meal she had prepared with loving care the previous evening had become dried up and horrible so she threw it in the bin. Another pang of sadness hit her and she remembered the positive thoughts she had when cooking it.

She boiled an egg and made toast. She opened the bottle of wine and poured a large glass for herself. Then she remembered. She took a sip and poured it down the sink. Her wine drinking days were over, at least for the next few months.

Jenny called during the evening.

'How are you now?' she asked.

'A bit better. Still weepy and emotional.'

'He's not back I take it?'

'No. Nobody's seen him. He's also been fired. He's missed too many shifts.'

'Heavens. And does that mean the caravan's going with his job? Do you have to move out?'

'Well, yes. Unless I take a permanent job at the hotel. The manager's offered me a receptionist's job. Says he's impressed with the way I handle things.'

'I should bloody well think so. You've been in the business since you could walk. So, will you take it?'

'I'm not sure. Rather too many memories. I was thinking I might go to the Cornish Hetherington for a spell. I needn't tell them anything more than my father asked me to visit for a while. Eventually I'll have to put my tail between my legs and go back home, but I still need time to come to terms with things.'

'Did you find any information from Jay's things?'

'Only that he pays a regular sum out of his bank account each month. Don't know where to, of course, but it's a standing order. Oh, and the manager said I wasn't the first woman to live in the caravan with him,' she added sadly.

'I bet Jay was delighted to discover you were worth something,' her friend said, voicing thoughts that had plagued Georgie for the last few days.

'Didn't make him stay though, did it? He still ran out on me.'

'I'll call you again in the morning. Try to get some sleep.'

'I will. Thanks again Jenny.'

She went for one last look outside and watched the last bus of the day draw in and leave its passengers.

No sign of the one person she was desperate to see. She shivered and wrapped herself in the duvet that still held traces of Jay's unique scent. She inhaled deeply, trying to recapture the magic she felt when he was lying next to her.

Exhausted with crying, worrying and indecision, she drifted into a deep sleep. It was hazy dawn when she roused and she sat up, wondering where she was for a moment. Reality came flooding back as did the feeling of nausea that went with her condition. When she had recovered slightly, she got up and ate yet more toast. She knew she must begin to eat a sensible diet but she needed to recover herself a little.

She looked at her reflection. Lank hair. Bleary eyes. She looked dreadful. She had a shower, washed her hair and put on some make-up. She was determined not to cry again and risked some mascara. Today was a day for making decisions. She took a deep breath and went down the hill to catch the bus.

Georgie sat in the hire car. It was a modest little car which would be economical to run. Now she had it, she couldn't quite decide where to go. On a whim, she drove into Redruth and stupidly drove round the streets, thinking she might see Jay. She went back to Poltoon, realising she was wasting her time. She parked outside the caravan and went inside. Someone had been there while she was away.

'Jay?' she called out hopefully. 'Jay, are you in here?' She flung open the bedroom door and saw the wardrobe on Jay's side had been cleared. She looked in the drawers. They were empty too. 'Damn, damn damn!' she called out. Why did he have to come when she was out? It was a disaster, the whole thing. He must have known she wasn't there.

161

So where had he been hiding? He must have seen her leave the village on the bus and come straight over to collect his things. Someone must have driven him. He couldn't have carried everything without transport. What a coward. He could at least have spoken to her. Furiously, she took out her phone and sent him a text.

Why? she typed. *Why did you do it this way? You might have said goodbye. I'm sorry your child will never know you but it will be your loss not his or hers. You're not the man I thought you were. Coward.*

She pressed send and sat down and cried all over again. Her phone rang and she snatched it, not looking at who was calling.

'Jay? Is that you?'

'Sorry love, it's Jenny.'

'Oh, hi. Sorry. I just sent Jay a text and thought he was responding. Stupid me. He's gone Jenny. Cleared his stuff out and gone.'

'Didn't he say anything?'

'He did it when I was out. I went to collect a hire car and he sneaked in right at that very time. I suspect he must have been watching and waiting for me to go. Someone must have driven him. He'd never have carried all his belongings himself.'

'Oh Georgie, I'm so sorry. Are you going to come and stay?'

'I'm not ready to leave just yet.'

'I'm really worried about you. You're sure

you won't do anything silly?'

'What, like driving round the streets of Redruth looking for him? I did that already. Silly me, I know.'

'You are in a state, aren't you? Look, I'll take the afternoon off tomorrow and drive down. I'll be with you by early evening. We can talk things through and maybe I can help you reach some sort of decision.'

'That's kind of you but I can't disrupt your life as well.'

'Rubbish. That's what friends are for. I can stay in the caravan, can't I?'

'Well, yes, I suppose so. Thanks Jenny. I'll see you then.'

'Make sure you eat properly and take care. See you soon.' Feeling a little more cheerful, she walked down to the village and went into the Beach Café. Audrey was delighted to see her.

'Come and sit down. I'll make us a pot of tea. Would you like a sandwich too? I bet you haven't been eating properly.'

'That would be lovely. Thank you. Oh, I've just realised, I've still got the T-shirt and cap. I'll wash it and bring it down later.'

'Don't worry. Drop it in sometime and I'll wash it when I do the rest of the things. Been very quiet here since you left.'

'As you say, the end of the season.'

'Now, tell me what's been going on? You don't look your usual cheery self.'

'Things haven't been going too well. Jay's left.'

'I did wonder. Got the sack has he?'

'Well, yes, I suppose so. We had a row and well, he just went off somewhere.'

'I thought I saw him in the village this morning. He was doing some shopping and then he drove up the hill. He was in a van. I didn't know he had one.'

'He doesn't. He must have borrowed it. He cleared his stuff out of the caravan.'

'Leaving you homeless? My offer of a room still stands if you want time to sort yourself out.'

'Thank you Audrey, that's good of you. I'm okay until next weekend, and then who knows ...'

'Come on now, eat up. I've got some nice fruit cake as well. Can't have you starving yourself.'

The kindly woman chatted on and Georgie half listened but was grateful for her offers of help. When the teapot was empty, she got up to clear the tray away.

'Leave it, dear. I'll see to it. Now then, hang on a minute and I'll get your envelope with your wages. I had it ready last night in case you called in.'

She went round the back of the counter and handed over a bulging envelope. 'I've put a bit of a bonus in. You've been such a good worker. If you want to come back next year, I'll be delighted to see you again.'

'Thank you very much. You've been lovely to work with. I don't think there's much chance I'll be this way again though.'

'Well the offer's there. And if you need a reference any time, just ask.'

It was a generous bonus under the circumstances and Georgie felt her emotions rise once more. She had at least proved one thing. She could stay with a boring job for a few months without a problem. She tucked the notes away safely and went back to her temporary home. There was a strange car waiting when she arrived back.

'Can I help?' she asked.

'Miss Hetherington?'

'Who's asking?'

'D C Thomas. I have some news for you about your car. Well, we have arrested the person behind the theft. We haven't recovered the vehicle yet but we hope to have the information we need soon.'

'Is it anyone we know?'

'I'm afraid so. It's your partner, Jay Jacobs, although perhaps he's your ex-partner now?'

'No . . . No, I don't believe it! He wouldn't do such a thing. In any case, he was with me when the car was stolen.'

'I'm sorry Miss Hetherington but he was definitely involved. He took a spare set of keys and passed them on to a friend of his, who then carried out the actual theft of the vehicle.'

'Life just gets better and better,' she muttered.

CHAPTER TWELVE

After the detective had left, Georgie slumped down and tried to come to terms with this latest blow. Her baby was going to be the child of a criminal. A memory of his face drifted across her imagination. How could someone like that be guilty of hurting her so much? She tried to hate him but each time a wave of anger crossed her, she melted again into a misery that was so new to her, she almost felt it in her very pulse beats.

He couldn't have done this. Not her Jay. Not the Jay she loved. There must be some terrible mistake. But then, she tried to reason, did she know him at all? Was the man she had fallen in love with, someone else entirely? How well did she really know him? It had only been three months or so. Could you ever really know anyone in so short a time?

She cooked some food and did her best to eat it, knowing her baby could suffer if she allowed herself to continue to wallow in self pity. She tried hard to make herself angry knowing that was a more positive emotion than feeling victimised. It worked briefly but not long enough to allow her to rest. There was a knock at the door. It was the duty manager.

'Hi Georgie. I was wondering if you are free to do a shift for me tomorrow? Our regular receptionist is off sick. You'd be helping me out. Unless you're working at your other job.'

'I'm not working but I'm not sure I can. I've been unwell.'

'I know you're upset. I also heard from the police about Jay. I was surprised actually. I didn't have him down as dishonest.'

'Yes, well as I now know it's hard to tell everything about a person at the start.'

'I hope you'll come in tomorrow. It might help distract you a little. Unless you have other things planned?'

'You're right. I need to do something. I have a friend coming down tomorrow evening. I hope it's okay if she stays with me?'

'Of course. I'm glad you'll have someone with you. We'll speak tomorrow. Thank you. Try and get some rest. You look absoluely worn out.'

*   *   *

In a way, work was almost something to look forward to. She was kept busy most of the next day. The manager came to ask for various tasks to be done and smiled approvingly at her obvious efficiency.

'You're doing well,' he told her. 'Are you

sure you don't want a permanent job?'

'I don't think so, but thank you.'

'So, where have you worked before?'

'Various places. Now, do you want me to do these spread sheets on the monthly occupancy?'

'If you know how to do it. Great. Thank you. But you need to take a break soon. Have you eaten?'

'I'll get a sandwich soon.'

'I'll phone the kitchen and get them to send some up for both of us. You can join me in the office in half an hour.'

'Well, okay. Thank you.' She settled back to her tasks. When the tray arrived, she went into the manager's office.

'So, how long have you known Jay?'

'Just through the summer.'

'You were fond of him, weren't you?'

'Oh yes. We gelled completely, or so I thought.'

'I'm sorry you've been hurt, but a clever, attractive lady like you will soon bounce back. I can sympathise. I've been through a break up myself not so long ago. You need to throw yourself into something absorbing and try to see there is still life to live. Think about the job I'm offering for instance.'

'I need to move on really. Too many bad memories here.'

'You might consider creating some new memories.' He smiled at her and reached out to take her hand. 'Find someone to take your mind off things.'

'Please, don't say any more. I'm certainly not ready to find someone new.' *And you'd be the very last person,* she thought. How could he? Her brain clicked into gear. He'd called her Georgie. He'd been on duty the day her parents had been there. He knew she was a Hetherington. That must be the reason for his sudden interest. He probably hoped she might help him get a better job. Her father had done a good job. She was suspicious of every man who came her way and even when she thought Jay didn't have any clue about her identity, it still went wrong. She had to face it. Guy was probably the only man on the planet who would have married her for herself. Even that was suspect. Now she was pregnant with another man's child, he wouldn't want her anyway.

'I'm sorry. That was tactless of me,' the manager was saying. 'I was really only trying to help.'

'Okay. Thanks. I'd better get back to the desk now. Thank you for the sandwiches.'

By the end of her shift, she felt weary. She glanced at her watch and dashed across to the caravan. She had left it in a mess and her friend would be here soon. They'd have to go out to eat that evening as there was nothing in the fridge to make a meal. She tidied up and rinsed the dirty dishes.

At least she looked a little more presentable today. The red eyes had calmed down and her nose looked less angry. She looked out as a car stopped and was delighted to see Jenny pulling up.

'Hello love. How are you?'

'Much better today, thanks. I've been working in the hotel. Oh, it's so good to see you,' she said hugging Jenny close.

'I take it you haven't heard anything more of Jay?'

Georgie frowned. 'Not exactly, but I had a visit from the police last night. It seems Jay has been arrested for being an accessory to the theft of my car. They say he took the spare keys and handed them to someone who stole it.'

'Good grief. I did wonder, but . . .'

'Well yes, but I can't believe he'd do something like that.'

'Depends how desperate he was feeling. How much do you truly know about his past?'

'Very little it seems. So many things are bugging me.'

'Like what?'

'When I told him I was pregnant, his comment was "no, not again" and then he said it couldn't be his because he couldn't have children.'

'It gets more weird by the minute. Do you think he already has a child? Or children, even?'

'I simply don't know anything any more. Strikes me that everyone was right. It's because I'm Georgina Hetherington, I'm only any use as a step up into a better job and lifestyle.'

'Don't be ridiculous. You're a lovely, warm and friendly person. And you're gorgeous too. Gosh, what I'd like to do to that man if I could get my hands on him.'

'I still can't help thinking there's something behind all this. I can't be such a rotten judge of character . . .'

'Don't try to excuse anything he's done. Being quite brutal about it, once he heard you were pregnant you didn't see him for dust. He doesn't want to take any responsibility. Plain and simple. Now, I for one am starving. I take it we're eating out as I don't smell any signs of cooking.'

'Yes. Sorry. I didn't have time to cook. Or anything to cook, come to that.'

'Well, my treat. Until you decide to go back home, you're going to need every penny you can save.'

They had a pleasant evening, though Jenny was soon losing patience as Georgie kept making excuses for Jay's behaviour.

'Have you asked at the hotel if they have Jay's address? Presumably he has money owing to him.'

'They wouldn't say. The only thing I was told was that he had a girlfriend living with him who worked in the kitchen. She came from Redruth. I even drove round the town looking for him. Ridiculous. Especially as he came here and cleared his stuff while I was out.'

'So maybe the police have some sort of information. If he was arrested, he's either in custody or they know where he is.'

'We could go to the police station in the morning and ask.'

'If you're sure you're up to it, Georgie. I don't want you getting upset all over again.'

'I haven't exactly stopped being upset. And the morning sickness isn't helping my mood, either.'

'I don't think I'd ever cope with being pregnant. I think I'll manage very well without children,' her friend remarked.

*   *   *

Feeling calmer than she had for a couple of days, Georgie managed to sleep reasonably well. After breakfast, Jenny asked if she still wanted to go to the police station.

'I think so. I need to do something, don't I?'

'And we need to discuss your options for the future. You can't seriously think you'll manage on your own with a baby?'

'I don't have to decide yet. I'll be able to work for ages yet and earn money.'

'Maybe, but you have to live. Rent

somewhere. Get baby stuff and clothes for both of you. Is it fair that you are depriving your baby of all the good things in life that money can buy? Imagine in a few years time, if ever he or she realises what he could have had.'

'Perhaps you're right but I can't face the recriminations, especially from my father. And if Jay is found guilty of this theft, that makes him a criminal. My life's a mess, isn't it?'

'Probably the worst mess you've ever made, but we'll find a way of dealing with it.'

'You think there is one?'

'There has to be. Come on. Dress yourself in your best outfit and we'll see if we can find this man who's made your life such a mess.'

They drove to the police station and saw the duty sergeant. Jay had not been detained and nor had he been charged. They didn't have enough evidence to make it stick, it seemed.

'Do you have an address for him?' Jenny asked. 'It's important that my friend contacts him urgently.'

'I'm sorry Miss. We can't give out that sort of information.'

'But he's . . . I must speak to him . . .'

'Sorry Miss. I can't help you.'

They turned away and Jenny said angrily, 'It isn't right, is it? Someone can just walk away and claim anonymity. They're not saying he isn't guilty, just that they can't prove it.'

'The officer who came round sounded very

positive too. I suppose until they find the actual car, there's little anyone can do. At least I've got the little hire car for a while.'

*   *   *

By the end of Jenny's stay, every angle had been talked about and discussed in depth. Georgie had still made no decision and had only four more days in the caravan, unless she took the receptionist's job. It would never work long term.

'I'm really going to have to leave you,' Jenny said. 'Sorry but I have important meetings tomorrow. I just wish you were closer to a decision.'

'I know. Thank you so much for being here for me. I'm reluctant to leave Cornwall without giving Jay one last chance to explain himself. I just know there has to be a reason for what he's done.'

'You shouldn't keep torturing yourself.'

'I know, but common sense has never been my strongest feature. Thanks again Jenny and safe journey back.'

She waved as her friend drove away and went back inside the lonely caravan that had been the scene of so much pleasure and joy until recently.

Two days to go and Georgie made a small decision. She would drive over to the Cornwall Hetherington. She could stay there for a few

174

days without her parents knowing and it might help her come to terms with her situation.

She had avoided answering the calls from her mother for several days, not trusting herself to keep her control. The last thing she wanted to do was to break down and confess all her problems over the phone.

'I shall be vacating the caravan tomorrow,' she informed the manager. 'Thank you for letting me stay on.'

'It's fine. Jay had paid for the rental till the end of the week. If you are in contact with him, we have a cheque for him for his final pay, and his official forms of course.'

'I'll let him know, but I doubt I shall be seeing him again.'

'I'm sorry. You look so sad. Shame it didn't work out but he clearly wasn't good enough for you.'

'Thank you. I'll bring the keys over tomorrow. I'm not absolutely sure what belongs to the hotel and what was Jay's. Linen and towels, that sort of thing.'

'Just leave whatever you're unsure about. Someone will sort it out. I'll have your pay cheque ready tomorrow too.'

'Thanks again.'

She spent the rest of the day clearing her things and packing them into the car. She felt as if this was the story of her life recently. Distinctly nomadic. She emptied the fridge and threw away what she couldn't eat.

Life at the Hetherington would be very different, even if it was only for a few days before her parents realised she was there. It was breathing space.

As Georgie drove into the car park, she was taken aback by the whole place. It was her first visit there and she realised it was one of the nicest of their hotels. With terrific views over the rugged north coast, it was a massive, elegant building. Once a Victorian holiday destination, it was grandeur on a scale unusual in this part of the country. She remembered her father buying the building and giving it a complete makeover and modernisation. She had seen the plans but the reality was spectacular. She hoped she would be recognised by someone in the management team because there was no way she could afford their prices in her current situation.

With a show of confidence she didn't really feel, she walked into reception and asked to see the manager. 'Who shall I say is asking for him?'

'Miss Georgina Hetherington. My father was staying here recently and I'm here to check on a few points he'd noticed were needing attention.'

'Miss Hetherington? I don't think we were informed of your arrival,' the receptionist said, looking slightly flustered.

'Of course you weren't. I was in the area and we decided on a spot check.'

'I'll see if the manager is available.'

Georgie walked over to a table carrying a range of newspapers and magazines and thumbed through them, looking for all the world as if she were checking on something.

'Miss Hetherington? James Willerby. I don't believe we've met before.'

'No. How do you do?'

'It's a pity we didn't know you were coming. We could have prepared for your arrival.'

'That loses the element of surprise, doesn't it?' she said with a smile.

'I suppose so, but I hope there's nothing wrong?'

'Not at all. My father likes to make occasional checks on things. He usually sends someone from head office but I was holidaying in the area so here I am. I trust you have a room available for me?'

'I . . . err . . . I'm sure we can arrange something. The main suites are occupied, I'm afraid, but we have a number of first class rooms. If you'll excuse me for a moment, I need to check on a few things. Can I get someone to bring you coffee?'

'Thank you. I'll wait here.'

She sat down and kept her fingers crossed that James wasn't calling her father to check up on her. If she was honest, she would expect him to make some sort of check before believing her.

She picked up one of the new brochures

from the rack on a side table and flicked through it. She had helped with the design and felt pleased with the look of the booklet. She paused and stared at the photograph inside. It was a picture of her standing in the doorway of one of the hotels with her mother and father. At least that would prove who she was, though she was currently looking far less well groomed than in the photo. Still, she had claimed to be on holiday. A session in the hotel salon would soon put that right.

A waiter arrived with her coffee. He glanced at the brochure she was holding.

'Oh, Miss Hetherington. Sorry, I didn't recognise you at first. Nice picture. Your parents were here recently.'

'That's right.' She smiled at him and sat down to drink her coffee. She hoped he'd make a comment to the manager to back up her story, but before he could James Willerby came back into reception.

'I'm sorry I didn't recognise you immediately, Miss Hetherington,' he said, blushing slightly.

Not to worry. We haven't met before and I do look rather, well, in holiday mode.'

'I have arranged a room for you. If you let me have your keys, I'll get someone to collect your luggage and take it to your room. Anything else I can do for you?'

'I'll meet with you later if that's convenient.'

'No problem. Your keys?'

Georgie hesitated. Her luggage was positively scruffy. A soft travel bag and numerous carrier bags. Hardly suitable for the Hetherington.

'I'll sort it out later, thank you.'

'If you'll just come to the desk, I'll sign you in.'

She went to her room. It was about four times the size of the caravan she had just left and with every luxury she could want. She sat on the bed and couldn't stop shaking. How could she find the confidence to behave as she had done? Something from deep down had re-emerged to the surface. She was Georgina Hetherington, daughter of the owners and heiress to a fortune. Maybe a day or two of her old life might give her the confidence to go back home.

She hoped nobody asked for any payment. She barely had enough for tips. Otherwise, her entire wages from the Beach Café would go in one night here. How stupid to move straight into the family hotel! What had she been thinking of? But now she was here, she had to keep up some sort of pretence. She went to the dining room and ordered her meal.

Alone again and out of the limelight, she was still the same messed up person. Pregnant, deserted and with a future more uncertain than ever. She needed to collect her scruffy luggage from the hire car. Damn, she thought. She was going to have to return the car to the garage. That meant driving back west to leave it there and she had no other transport to go anywhere after that. Did being pregnant stop everyone from functioning normally? Or was it just her that had a brain that appeared to have turned to porridge?

'Oh Jay, what have you done to me?' she murmured.

She allowed herself to think of him as she had known him. Caring, wonderful and a lover that only came in dreams. A once in a lifetime meeting. She would never love anyone else like she loved him. She would probably never dare to love anyone else at all. Was that it for her whole life? She had the training behind her to be a business woman. Once her child reached school age, she would be free to work when she wanted to. But that was years away. Years and years. How could she cope alone with pregnancy and a small baby for the coming months? Life was just a series of questions—of unknowns—and she was ill-equipped to deal with any of it.

Later the manager called her.

'What time would you like to schedule our meeting? I have to see staff members for our weekly briefing.'

Georgie was stumped. She had no idea what she wanted to say in any case and felt as if the whole charade was about to crumble around her.

'I'll tell you what,' she said. 'Why don't I sit

in on your meeting? That will give me an idea of what goes on and how it all works.'

'Oh, well if you like. Four o'clock suit you? That's our normal time, before prep for evening service begins.'

'Fine. Just do your normal thing. No special recognition for me please.'

She put the phone down and hoped she had sounded convincing.

*   *   *

The day dragged on. The meeting was interesting and everything seemed to run so well she really had no excuse for being there.

She stayed for another day, enjoying the change after her weeks of living on very little money. But it came to her that she would always prefer to be poor and with Jay than rich without him. But it was not an option any more. Jay was no longer in her life and she must move on. Do the best for her baby and herself. She would leave the hotel in the morning and look for a job. Staying in Cornwall was her first choice and if that didn't work out, she would think about returning home to her parents. The phone rang.

'Good evening Madame. You have visitors in reception. I can send them up or you may prefer to come down.'

'Who is it?'

'I've been asked not to say. It's a surprise.'

Puzzled, she tidied herself up and went downstairs.

'Mummy? Jenny? What on earth are you doing here?'

'We've come to try and persuade you to come home with us,' Jenny said sheepishly.

'Oh Jenny, how could you? You promised me you wouldn't say anything.'

'I didn't. Your mother found out you were here and asked me to come with her.'

'Is Daddy here too?'

'No. I felt it better to come without him. I called Jenny and she agreed to drive me down.'

'But how did you know I was here, in the hotel?'

'Shall we go and sit somewhere in private to discuss all of this? I don't think the main reception area is quite the place.' Jenny was noticing people starting to stare. They went into one of the small lounges and shut the door.

'I'm afraid a Hetherington can't stay in one of the hotels without someone letting it slip. Someone called the office. Daddy's PA called me and said she'd keep it from Daddy. He is still furious with you. I thought there'd be more chance of reasonable discussion if I came alone and a better chance if Jenny was with me.'

'It's good of you Jenny. You could hardly have got home after your last visit.'

'I'm worried about you. I didn't want you making stupid decisions, not when you're so vulnerable.'

'So what have you told my mother?'

'Just that Jay has left, and that he is suspected of being involved in the theft of your car.'

She stared at her friend. Had she said anything about the pregnancy? Jenny gave an almost imperceptible shake of her head, unnoticed by Georgie's mother.

'I'm so sorry my darling. He was a lovely man but clearly not good enough for you. You know what your father is always saying . . .' Her mother paused.

'Oh yes, indeed. Nobody could possibly love me for myself. Only for the money and job prospects. I realise all of that. That's why I thought I was safe with Jay but he still left me for being myself,' she said with tears stinging her eyes.

'Don't sound so bitter Georgie. Your father has always wanted what is best for you. He only wants to protect you.'

'That's right, and look what happened when I made a break for it. Oh, I'm sorry. I know you want to help, but I've decided, I'm going to stay in Cornwall. It's a good place to live and I've been happy here. Well, most of the time. I'll get a job.'

'Oh Georgie, do you have to? Why not come home and work for the hotel near us if that's what you want to do.'

'But don't you see? Daddy would still be on my back. No, there are plenty of hotels in Cornwall. I can find a job.'

'I tell you what. If you're determined to stay in Cornwall, why not work here for a while? There's sure to be something. That way, we'll be sure you're looked after properly.'

'You'd be safe and you'd have a decent room to stay in,' Jenny put in.

'I'd made up my mind to move on,' she hesitated. 'But it might work . . . But will I be able to do a proper job without everyone thinking I'm spying on them? They seem like a good team. I wouldn't want to spoil anything.'

'It sounds like a brilliant idea,' Jenny agreed. 'You getting properly fed and the baby would be much—'

'What do you mean?' Mrs Hetherington said in horror.

'Sorry!' Jenny spluttered. 'Oh, I'm really sorry!'

'You mean she's pregnant? Oh my god, no! Oh Georgie, how could you?'

'Nature, Mother. You know how it works.'

'But with a . . . a criminal. I don't know what your father will say, Georgina.'

'I think I do. So it's best if you say nothing and let me get on with my life. Working here for a while is a good idea but when I get nearer the time, I'll quietly disappear and find some way of managing. Now, if you'll excuse me, I need to go to bed.'

'No you don't, my girl. Just stay exactly where you are. I can't believe you knew, Jenny? And you didn't tell me?' Mrs Hetherington spluttered.

'I was torn between being a loyal friend and responsible. I'm sorry, but it wasn't my place to tell you. That was a stupid slip of the tongue. I'm sorry.'

'Well this news certainly changes everything. You'll have to come back with us. Whatever your father says, this is our grandchild we are talking about. You'll never manage on your own and indeed, why should you? Every child deserves a decent start in life.'

'I need more time,' Georgie insisted.

'Let's sleep on it. I've booked us a couple of rooms. We'll meet at breakfast and talk again then.'

'All right, Mummy. But don't expect me to do anything I don't believe in.' She stood hesitantly, unsure of how she was supposed to react. Jenny broke the tension and gave her a hug. Her mother glared but gave her a hug too but Georgie could feel it was merely a token gesture.

She lay awake for much of the night, tossing things round and round. It was becoming a habit.

*   *   *

185

Jenny knocked on her door early next morning.

'Can I come in? Or don't you want to speak to me ever again?' Her friend looked miserable.

'I suppose she had to find out sooner or later but it was all a bit sudden.'

'I'm so sorry. I thought if I was here it might ease things a bit and then I do something stupid. I take it you've heard nothing else of the man himself?'

'Seems he's disappeared off the planet, but I think I realise that I'm better off without him.'

'You'll be safe here, and your mum will help you sort things out Might make your life easier. You'll get paid too.'

'I s'pose. So much for being independent. I wanted to find my own way through this mess. I'd better face up to her over breakfast. Hey, I haven't been sick today. Maybe that's one stage over with.'

'Do you know how far on you are?'

'Not really. It can't be more than two and a bit months.'

'Haven't you seen a doctor yet?'

'When have I had time for all that? You were only here a couple of days ago.'

'Then that's your next priority. Make sure you do it. Or we'll stay on and make you go.'

'Okay. Promise. It just makes everything seem so real. How will I cope with being a mother, Jenny? It's such a shock.'

'You'll cope, when the time comes. Come on. Breakfast.'

It was a tense meal but at least with so many people around, there was no chance of a heated discussion. Mrs Hetherington seemed reasonable and took the attitude that staying on good terms was better than losing her daughter altogether.

'I'm going to give you a credit card for emergencies but please be sensible. You can buy what you need. It's one of my private ones I have in reserve and Daddy won't know anything about it. You'll also need a car. I shall try to get Daddy's PA to clarify matters with the insurance. You can't go on like this. It's ridiculous. Keep this hire car and I'll let you know the situation. Now, promise to see a doctor and follow any advice you get and you must also promise to answer my calls. None of this hedging. Honesty, from now on.'

'Thank you, Mummy. You're very generous. I'll do my best to manage but it will be nice to know that you're on my side.'

'Oh no, I'm not. Not in any way. I'm horrified by the whole thing but you're my only daughter and I can't abandon you, whatever you've done. It's up to you to organise work here.' She got up and left the table. Jenny stared at her friend.

'That all sounds reasonable, don't you think?'

'I guess so. Yes, of course it does. I am still

being organised to some extent, but I suppose I'm out of Daddy's reach and of course, I still have this baby growing inside me—and I still miss Jay. I can't help it but I love him. I'm trying hard not to.' She felt tears burning once more.

'Your hormones are all over the place. You've got to forget him Georgie. You have to get on with your life now. Come on. You've only known him for three or four months. You've lived all the rest of your life without him.'

'I know, you're right, but he's still the best thing that ever happened to me. He made me discover myself in a way that was completely new. I'm glad I'll have a part of him forever,' she said as she touched her stomach.

'You're letting yourself wander into some fantasy world Georgie. He's gone. Now, come on. Help me pack. We're driving straight back this morning. I have to get back to work.'

Georgie watched them drive away and went back inside. She had to organise a job and move into staff quarters rather than the guest room. It was about to become an even more difficult morning she thought.

Explanations were tricky. Despite the idea that nepotism would not come into the sort of job she would do, the manager was not comfortable with her tackling any menial jobs.

'I think I'd better make you a sort of personal assistant to me and other senior staff.

You are familiar with all of the systems. I understand you helped set them up.'

'Well, yes, I did. But I don't expect any favouritism.'

'I can't have you working in the kitchen. It makes sense for you to do something you're good at. It will be of great help to me too. I'll have to move you into one of the staff rooms, though.'

'I expected that. If it's convenient I'd like to start properly in a couple of days. I have a few things I need to organise.'

'That's perfect. I'll arrange office space for you and we'll sort out a room. Thank you Miss Hetherington.'

'Please, call me Georgie.'

'Georgie it is then.'

'Thank you, James. May I call you that?'

'Of course. We're fairly informal amongst ourselves. Perhaps not in front of the rest of the staff, though.'

'Okay, but please let me be Georgie to everyone. I don't want the staff constantly reminded of who I am.'

'Your photograph is in the brochures so it won't be a secret.'

'I know, but I don't want to push it. Now I wonder if you could tell me where the nearest doctor is? I need to register.'

'I can call the hotel doctor if there's something wrong.'

'No. There's nothing wrong but I do need to

register.'

He gave her a card with various local information. She put it in her pocket. She needed to buy some more clothes for working and set off to the nearby town. She found the doctor's surgery and went to sign in.

'Do you need to see a doctor now?'

'Well, if possible.'

'Can you come back in half an hour? One of our lady doctors will be free.'

'That's wonderful. Thank you.'

Things were coming together nicely. She wandered into the High Street and saw there were several shops selling clothing. She looked into a charity shop window and saw a number of items of baby things. If all else failed, it was useful to know she could get such things.

The doctor was helpful and gave her a handful of leaflets explaining what she needed to do.

'And you've really no idea when it might be due? When was your last period?'

Georgie shook her head.

'I'm not entirely sure. Everything's been something of a muddle lately. I didn't even realise I could be pregnant until I did a test. Even that was after I'd been sick a few times.'

'The first thing is to organise a scan and then we'll have some idea of your due date. I'll arrange it right away.'

'Thank you, doctor.'

As she left, it hit her hard. This baby was

becoming more and more of a reality.

'Oh Jay. What have we done?'

CHAPTER THIRTEEN

Jay walked into the huge reception area of the Hetherington Hotel and looked around. The place was intimidating in its grandeur. He'd known it was a five star rating but was taken aback by the magnificence of the building. And to think, the heiress to all of this had shared a caravan with him. He drew himself up straight and took a deep breath, walking to the reception with an air of confidence he did not feel.

'Can I help you sir?' the receptionist said, smiling at the handsome man with more than her usual enthusiasm.

'I wondered if Miss Georgie Hind is staying here?'

'I'm afraid not sir. We have no one of that name registered.'

'She may be using her other name. Georgina Hetherington?'

The girl looked up from her computer screen in surprise. 'I can't give out that information sir.'

'So she is here.'

'I didn't say that. I merely said that we don't give out the names of any of our guests.'

'But it's vital I contact her as soon as possible. It's a very urgent matter.'

'What makes you think she is here?'

'Just a hunch. She left her previous job and I think this is where she would have moved to next.'

'You could leave a message and if she does contact us, we could pass it on. Can I ask your name?'

'Never mind. I'll stay around for a while longer and perhaps I'll meet her.'

'Shall I say who was asking for her?'

'That's another way of asking my name. I might try to contact her by phone. Thanks for your help.' *I don't think.*

He went outside and wandered down the imposing drive. The gardens were looking wonderful with plenty of early autumn colour. Though the Clarence Hotel was nice, it came nowhere near to this standard. He sat on a seat outside the walls and looked at the sea. He would stay there for a while and see if Georgie returned. It was probably a hopeless cause even trying to provide some sort of explanation. He'd never met anyone like Georgie before. Now he knew why, he thought, looking back at this hotel.

There were several Hetheringtons around the country, probably all as splendid as this one. He was totally out of his depth in her world and if he'd known from the start who she was, he'd have been far too inhibited to speak to her. After a couple of hours, he gave up and went into town. It was pointless trying to speak to Georgie. He had done far too many things wrong for her to forgive him. He had been stupid and destroyed the only true love of his life. He drove away in the borrowed van and decided it was time to make himself a new life. He had finally untangled the mess he had created in his past and now he had to move on. Perhaps he could visit his sister. She would surely give him a temporary home for a while.

*   *   *

Georgie drove back into the hotel drive a few moments after he had left.

'Has Mr Willerby assigned me a new room yet do you know?'

'I believe so. He's in the office. I'll give him a buzz. Oh, a gentleman was asking after you. I didn't confirm you were staying here. I hope I did the right thing?'

'What sort of gentleman?'

'Well, if I'm honest, a gorgeous looking gentleman. Very tall. Dark hair. Amazing greenish eyes, or they might have been brown . . .' Georgie went pale.

'Did he leave any message?' she stammered.

'No. He wouldn't give his name. Said something about contacting you by phone.'

'Thanks,' she said absently, though Georgie

had banned Jay's number for coming through on her phone.

'If he calls again?'

'I simply don't know. Actually, let me know but don't confirm that I am here.'

'I see. Leave it with me.' The receptionist, sensing some juicy gossip, had a glint in her eye. What with Mrs Hetherington coming down last night and then leaving first thing . . . and Georgie starting to work here . . . it all looked highly suspicious.

James came into reception and gave her the number of her new room. The staff rooms were quite small compared to the guest rooms but still provided comfortable accommodation. Georgie was given a room with en-suite. No nepotism of course, she thought.

She settled in, trying hard not to think about Jay possibly close by. Would she see him if came to the hotel again? Was he here because it was her family's hotel or did he have an explanation for his dreadful behaviour? Did she want to see him or would it merely be rubbing salt into her already bleeding wounds? She tried to be objective. He was certainly everything she could have wanted physically but he was a liar and a thief. He was a coward, especially leaving her the way he did. She remembered the lovely times they had shared. She thought of his gentle care for her at times and his humour at others. But when it had mattered most, he had run out on her. She knew exactly what her friend Jenny would say. *Don't do it. Let him go. Forget him.*

'Good advice,' she muttered to herself. She should do all of those things but would she have the strength to follow it through? Perhaps he wouldn't come again, anyway. She'd just have to follow her instincts if he did.

It seemed pointless to drift around so she decided to begin work the next day. She went to the desk she had been assigned and began to familiarise herself with the tasks she was to take on. James spent some time with her and gave her a few jobs to do, jobs that she knew were non-essential, trivial things. She looked up whenever the bell rang on reception, wondering if Jay would show his face again.

Jenny sent an email asking how things were going. She replied that Jay had been looking for her and her friend immediately phoned.

'You can't seriously think of speaking to him. Georgie, for heaven's sakes. You'll be asking for more heartache.'

'I know. I know all of that, but I still need some sort of explanation. I've been over and over it in my mind and I have to know what I did that was so wrong. What did he mean by his words when I told him about the baby?'

'You're torturing yourself over and over again. Georgie. Get on with your life and make the most of it. You're a lovely young woman. You'll be a mother with a gorgeous baby soon. Settle for that for now. I'll call you later.'

'Okay Jenny. Thanks again for caring.'

*   *   *

Georgie settled into a routine of working, though she doubted her broken heart would ever heal. The other staff were becoming aware of her condition and although curious, respected her status in the hotel hierarchy and said nothing to her face.

As Christmas approached she had a noticeable bump which she no longer tried to hide. By her due date in March she would be larger still. She was no nearer knowing what to do when the time came. She had spells of misery that occasionally drove her near to despair. The thought of her unborn child kept her going.

Her mother called regularly and though often sounding distant, was still offering some support.

'Are you thinking of coming home for Christmas?' she asked halfway through December.

'I don't know. How would Daddy be about seeing me in this state?' she asked.

'Not at all comfortable but he has to know soon. I know that I promised to keep it from him for now, but I don't want to go on deceiving him. I can break it to him. I'd like to see you, anyway.'

'I do miss you, Mummy. I'm sorry about

everything.' She broke down and once more tears flowed in a way she was getting used to. She tried to blame the hormones, as ever. 'I'll have to go, Mummy. Sorry.'

Christmas. Here at the hotel it would be crazy busy. Hetherington Hotels made a big feature of seasonal activities and Christmas breaks for large numbers of guests. Perhaps staying for all of that would be the best thing she could do. It would take her mind off what she was missing at home and the changes in her life since last year. She wondered where Jay was and what he would be doing for Christmas. She forced her thoughts away from him. She allowed herself to think of him just twice a day but it was hard to stick to.

On one of her rare days off, she had driven back to Poltoon but it had been a disastrous visit. The Beach Café was shuttered up and the beaches deserted apart from a few hardy locals who were surfing. She shivered and drove away.

She had been tempted to go for a coffee at the Clarence Hotel but had resisted. If Jay had returned to work there, she could never have coped with meeting him in public. She drove around Redruth again, thinking she might catch a glimpse of him walking round the streets. Futile. Stupid. She cursed herself all the way back to the safety of the Hetherington. Would she ever get over him?

As expected, the Christmas period was

frantic. She worked harder than she had ever worked in her life and by the time January was into double figures, she was near collapse. James Willerby took her to one side.

'I think you need to take a break. In your condition, and working at the rate you have been, you'll be damaging your baby as well as yourself. Why don't you go home to your parents?'

'Has my mother been talking to you?'

'No, of course not, but I can see you are exhausted. My wife could never have kept working the way you've been doing all these weeks when she was expecting our first child.'

'I didn't realise you had a family. How dreadful of me. I've been so wound up in my own troubles, I never even asked.'

'That's all right. I try to keep home and work separate anyway. Look, if you'd like to talk to my wife, I'm sure she'd be happy to answer any question you might have about birth and babies and so on.' He gave her a phone number and urged her to call. The next day she went to the Willerbys' home for coffee.

'You know, the one thing that helped me most was having James around and the support of my mum and dad.' Sarah Willerby was a lovely lady with two little children playing happily around her feet. 'I'm not trying to pry in any way but you mustn't think of trying to cope on your own. You have resources behind you and whatever the circumstances, parents who will certainly care when the time comes.'

'I suppose so. Thank you. I'm still wallowing a bit. As you suspect, the father of my baby has let me down badly. I won't be seeing him again.'

'I'm sorry. But you have friends. Don't underestimate the importance of that. Your emotions will be all over the place whatever happens.'

'As if they're not already,' she replied with a grimace. 'But thanks for the advice.'

A few days later, she telephoned her mother.

'Mummy? I think I need to come home. Can you let me know if it will be all right? When you've spoken to Daddy of course.'

'He knows already. I told him over Christmas. I just couldn't keep it to myself any longer. I think he's getting used to it now. Naturally, he blew his top when he heard of the circumstances but you will be welcome here. There's something else you should know. Jenny has got engaged. She didn't want to tell you for fear of upsetting you but I said I'd tell you when I spoke to you next.'

'That's silly. She should have told me. I'm happy for her. I'll give her a call.'

'When do you think you'll come?'

'I'll finish this week out and come down at the beginning of next. Thanks for everything, Mummy.'

'You're still my daughter but I don't want you to think everything will be all right from now on. There are many bridges to rebuild.'

'I know. I'll see you soon.'

She gave notice to James who looked relieved.

'You've worked hard but I'm pleased you are going home. You couldn't continue working here with a new baby.'

*   *   *

It was impossibly difficult to leave Cornwall. Georgie felt as if she was cutting off every link to Jay and the happiness she had known. Where was he now? What was he doing with his life? Perhaps he had taken up a life of real crime and could even be in prison. Nothing had ever been heard of her sports car again. Whatever his part in the theft, she had heard no more.

Sadly, she packed her things and drove away. She had been given gifts of baby things by the staff and good wishes had gone with her. She had been touched by the sincerity but couldn't help wondering if it was because of who she was.

Nervously, Georgie went into the home she had known all her life. It was one of the most difficult things she'd had to do during this whole thing. Her mother greeted her with a hug, but it felt a little strained.

'I hope you had a good journey dear,' she said.

'Not bad. It seemed a long way.'

'You look tired.'

'I am. I was tired before I left and the journey on top of it was a bit much. I'd like to go to my room and freshen up, if that's all right. I suppose Daddy isn't back yet?'

'No. He's away this evening so we'll have time to catch up.' Her mum glanced at her bump. 'You look as if you haven't too long to go.'

'It's due in March. Around the middle of the month.'

'Oh dear. I suppose we shall have to organise doctors and hospitals and things.'

'I suppose so.'

'And you've had no more contact with the father?'

'Nothing. Have you heard anything about the car theft?'

'Nothing at all. As far as I know, nobody was charged. An unsolved crime, I'm afraid. Anyway, go and get yourself sorted out. Dinner will be ready in an hour.'

It felt like being a guest in some stranger's home, Georgie thought. This was going to be a difficult time. At least she didn't have to face her father just yet.

She looked round her pretty bedroom and smiled at seeing her things again. She opened her wardrobe and looked at the long rails of clothes she'd almost forgotten. Nothing was going to fit her for the next few weeks. Would she ever feel like wearing them again?

She unpacked her collection of things from Cornwall and hung them up. She put the baby clothes into a drawer and closed it firmly. She didn't want to think about it just yet.

'Dinner's ready,' her mother said, knocking on the door before opening it.

'Thanks, Mummy. Just coming.'

Gradually the tension was easing as the two women, who were once so close, drew closer once more.

'Do you know what it is yet?' her mother asked. 'I know they seem able to tell these days.'

'It's a boy. I hoped that might please Daddy. A new Hetherington male in the dynasty.'

'But it's not a Hetherington, is it? That's the whole problem.'

'He will be. There's no point acknowledging the father, is there? He didn't want to know.'

'Come on. Eat up. You need proper nutrition.'

Later as they were clearing away the dishes, her mother paused, then turned towards her.

'Guy's been asking after you,' she said casually. 'He wants to come and see you.'

'Really? I'd have thought I'd be the last person he wanted to see again.'

'He's very fond of you. He knows about the baby but he still wants to see you.'

'This terrible scarlet woman, you mean?'

'No need to be like that. He's coming for drinks tomorrow evening. Daddy won't be back for another day or two but he called earlier to see if you were home.'

Once she was on her own again, Georgie reflected on the evening. So, Guy was still around and wanted to see her. She couldn't help but wonder why. Surely he couldn't still want to marry her? He had taken her rejection very well at the time, almost as if he expected it. Now she was carrying another man's baby, he'd be an idiot to consider marrying her. Perhaps he was as business minded as her father and thought the merger between their families was worth it. Was that any good reason to marry someone? Not in her book.

CHAPTER FOURTEEN

Guy arrived at the house promptly at six o'clock, as arranged. He was dressed in his dark business suit with a discreet silk tie and matching shirt. Georgie greeted him nervously, not sure whether to shake his hand or kiss his cheek. He leaned forward and kissed her.

'Good to see you again, Georgie. You're looking very well.'

'Thank you. Nice to see you,' she added politely.

'I . . . I was glad to hear you were returning home. I missed you.' She didn't know how to reply and busied herself pouring drinks. Her mother came into the room.

'Oh good. You've organised the drinks. I'm sorry I wasn't here to greet you. Crisis in the kitchen but all is now well. So how are you getting on Guy? Is all going smoothly at the Westland group?' she asked.

'Not bad. Though we're somewhat down on profits at the moment. Recession is biting us hard.'

Georgie was half listening as the conversation droned on with business, business and more business. If they were married, life would be one long discussion of profits and losses: how to improve facilities . . . it would be like their parents' marriages. Boring and tedious with only one thing in common. She watched her mother reacting with the man and could see that they were friends and almost like colleagues.

'So what do you think Georgie?' her mother asked suddenly.

'Sorry? I was miles away.'

'Guy was asking if you'd like to go out for dinner with him?'

'Thank you but I thought you had dinner organised here.'

'Tomorrow?' Guy asked.

'Of course she would, wouldn't you darling?'

'Thank you. That's very kind of you.' She

didn't know how to refuse. It was as if her entire thought processes had turned to mush. She just knew she would spend the next day wondering how to get out of it. He left at seven precisely. What a well organised life he led.

Mrs Hetherington insisted on taking Georgie shopping the next day.

'You can't keep wearing those maternity jeans and that scruffy shirt. Haven't you got anything else?'

'Just the business suit I was wearing for work.'

'Well you can't go out with Guy looking like a rag bag. We'll go to that nice boutique we used to use.'

'If you like, but it's only a few more weeks till my old things will fit again. I don't want to waste money.'

'Don't be silly. You're home now. You don't have to skimp and scrape any more. And we shall have to start looking for baby things. Oh dear, it's becoming more and more real each day. I'm going to become a grandmother. I simply wasn't expecting it to happen quite so soon.'

'I can always go away again and find somewhere to live and spare you the shame of it all.'

'Don't be silly dear. I don't think you realise how much support you'll need.'

Georgie shrugged and allowed herself to be led into the shop. She felt disinterested in the clothes she was shown and didn't even look at the price tags. If her mother wanted to organise it, she would let her. It was all back to normal . . . she was being manipulated just as she always had been.

'Can we go home now please? I'm feeling rather tired.' With a frown, her mother agreed and collected the carrier bags to take back to the car.

'I thought we might look in the baby department and we need to decide which room we shall make into a nursery. We shall have to engage some sort of nursemaid too, so she will also need a room nearby.'

'Oh, for goodness' sake, Mummy. I can pick up a second hand pram when I need it. I've got some baby clothes the staff gave me before I left. That's enough to be going on with. I don't want a nursemaid either. I'll look after my baby.'

She went to her room for the rest of the afternoon. Feeling guilty about her behaviour, she got ready for her dinner with Guy and put on one of the new dresses her mother had bought.

It was a tense meal. Guy did his best to avoid mentioning the baby growing inside her. When they had eaten their dessert, he reached into his pocket and laid a small box in front of her. 'What's this?' she asked.

'Open it and see.' He was smiling and reached over to open it for her, when she sat

206

staring at the box without moving. 'Georgie, I still want to marry you. If we do it soon, nobody will realise it isn't my child. I'll bring it up as my own and I promise I won't ask any questions.'

'Oh Guy, you are such a nice man. Thank you for asking me and it's very generous of you under the circumstances.'

'I'm not listening to the "but" that's coming. All our parents agree it is the best solution for you and the baby. I'm very fond of you. We've practically grown up together so there's no doubt we get on well. I hope you'll take the ring and wear it.' He took it out of the box and slipped it onto her finger.

'It's very pretty,' she said at last. 'Thank you.'

That was it. Evidently, they were now engaged. Where were the violins? The racing heart beats? The romance? The love?

'Come on. Let's go back home.'

When they arrived, she saw her father's car parked outside. She closed her eyes, knowing she was about to face the roaring tiger that was her father when things weren't going his way.

Guy took her hand and led her inside. He smiled and nodded to the reception committee comprising both her parents and Guy's. He held out Georgie's left hand to display the engagement ring. Champagne corks popped and the celebration and congratulations began.

Georgie seemed to be somewhere floating

above the assembly, remote and out of it all.

'We're thinking of a small private ceremony very soon and we can have a proper celebration in a few months.'

'After the bastard is born you mean?' Georgie's words were flung out of nowhere, her emotions in shreds. She rushed from the room, leaving everyone standing in confusion.

'Leave her,' Mrs Hetherington said. 'I suspect it's the hormones reacting.'

Far from accepting congratulations and celebrating, she felt life was filled with impending disaster. She was being organised into a safe marriage with undoubtedly, a generous man who really cared for her. She couldn't bear to hurt him, the man she felt as close to as a brother, but marrying him would be so wrong for both of them. When Jay's son was born, he would have dark hair, remarkable green (or were they brown?) eyes. Everyone would know immediately he couldn't be the child of two blond, blue-eyed parents.

She lay face down on her bed, her body wracked by sobs. Will this misery ever end she asked herself over and over?

*　　　*　　　*

The date for the wedding had been set for the following week. The first of February was agreed by the four parents and Guy. Georgie said little and allowed herself to be taken to

208

buy a dress for the ceremony and settle for a meal at a local restaurant. Her friend Jenny would be there and the parents but nobody else. A grand party was arranged for the end of March when guests from everywhere would arrive at the largest of the hotels for a party to end all parties.

'You're happy with this?' Jenny asked the night before the wedding day. 'Only you look as if you're going to the guillotine rather than the registry office.'

'Or Jane Eyre about to discover the mad woman in the attic. Only I'm the mad woman.'

'You don't have to go through with it you know.'

'You just try thwarting my parents. Daddy has actually treated me almost as human since the engagement. He's got his way, don't you see? A satisfactory business arrangement. No, I'll have to go through with it. I had my fling and tasted what love is all about. Now I have to suffer the consequences.'

'Oh Georgie. I'm so sorry.' She hugged her friend and wished with all her heart that this wedding day could be everything Georgie had dreamed of.

*   *   *

The ceremony, such as it was, would take place at midday that day. It seemed many people had heard about it and her mother

209

came into her room with a large heap of letters and cards. She went through them in a desultory fashion. There was a large envelope with the insignia of the Cornish Hetherington Hotel. She opened it, expecting a card signed by members of the staff but instead, with a compliments slip, there was a sealed letter. The slip stated that the letter had been hand delivered the previous week and was being forwarded in case it was important. Her hands shook as she recognised Jay's writing. She hesitated, wondering if she should tear it up or open it.

My Darling Georgie, she read. Tears filled her eyes and she could scarcely see the rest of the words.

I realise you probably don't want to read this or have any contact with me but I have to explain things to you. I wanted and prayed to see you face to face but I could never find you. I tried to look for you at the hotel but they wouldn't tell me if you were even there. I am sending this in the hope that it will reach you eventually. I tried to phone but I was told your number could not accept my call. You must hate me so very much, but there are reasons for my behaviour, reasons you will undoubtedly find hard to understand. I am now going to work in Hertfordshire, just so that I might possibly be closer to you and even see you again. If you have continued with the pregnancy, it must be nearing the time when our child is due. I'm begging you to speak to me. I want to know how you are and if you can forgive me in any way. I'd like to be a part of the baby's life.

Please, I'm begging you, call me and allow me to explain. I love you Georgie. I love you with all my heart. Jay. xxx

Jenny came into the room and sat on the bed.

'What's wrong love? Why are you crying?'

Georgie handed her the letter and Jenny read it quickly. 'Wow, talk about timing! Can you believe it? Fancy it arriving this morning of all times. It was dated a week ago.'

'It was sent on from the hotel. I don't know what to do.'

'Do you want to listen to him or shouldn't you rip it up and get on with the day as planned.'

'He loves me Jenny. He says he still loves me.'

'Of course he does. You haven't learned a thing, have you? Remember what everyone has said to you. He discovered who you really are and everything changed.'

'He said he loved me way before he knew who I was.'

'You're sure of that?'

'Of course I am.'

'But it's too late now; you're marrying Guy at noon.'

Georgie flung back the bedclothes and reached for her phone. She dialled Jay's number and sat back down on the bed. 'There's a whole four hours for me to listen to what he says.'

Jenny left the room discreetly. She hesitated. Should she report the latest turn of events to Mrs Hetherington or let things take their course? She decided not to interfere.

'Jay? It's me.'

'Oh Georgie! Thank God! Thank you for calling. I've been waiting all these days and had almost given up hope.'

'I've only just got your letter.'

'How are you?'

'We're both well.'

'Both? Does that mean you've had our child?'

'Not yet. I have a few weeks to go, but he's growing nicely. I'm in good health and everything is normal.'

'Oh Georgie,' he said again. 'I'm so delighted. Can we meet soon? I need to tell you everything.'

'It will have to be very soon. I'm getting married at midday.'

'Married? Who on earth are you marrying?'

'Guy of course. The dynastic arrangement that will make our parents so happy.'

'You can't Georgie! You mustn't marry him. Where are you? I'm coming over right away. I'm only a few miles from your home. I assume that's where you are.'

'I'll meet you. There's a wood on the side of

the road near the house. About a mile away. I'll wait there in half an hour.'

CHAPTER FIFTEEN

Georgie showered and dressed in her old jeans and a loose top. Everyone was in the dining room eating breakfast but she sneaked past the door without being seen. She drove out as quietly as she could, knowing that they would try to stop her if she was seen. Her heart was beating wildly as she pulled into the track off the road and waited. Would he find the place from her sparse instructions? She stood near the road, ready to dodge back if anyone came looking for her. After what seemed like an eternity, she saw a small van coming towards her and stared to see if it could be Jay. He gave a wave and drove to where she indicated. He rushed to her the moment he stopped and pulled her into his arms. She felt as if her legs could no longer support her as the emotions surged through her body. This was what love should be like.

'Oh Jay! It's so good to see you.'

'Really?' he murmured. 'I was so scared that you'd hate me forever. I can't tell you how sorry I am. Come and sit in the van. You're shivering.'

She allowed herself to be led to sit inside

the little van. 'Can I kiss you?' he asked. She smiled and pulled him close.

'You'd better start talking first.' She needed to be rational and not allow her emotional responses to take over.

'I should begin with my reaction to your saying you were pregnant. I had a girlfriend for a couple of years who announced she was pregnant. I believed her and went along with what she said. When she was nearing the time, she told me it wasn't mine. I was gutted. After the baby was born, it seemed the other man, whose child it really was, disappeared and she was left alone to struggle. I've been supporting them since, as much as I could afford to. I gave up my college course and worked all hours, as you know, to keep making payments to Laurie for the baby. She kept calling me to ask for help and I had to go and see her. That's why I kept disappearing on the bus. I hated lying to you about that but she threatened such awful things that she would do to herself or the baby. I finally decided that I couldn't go on any longer, because of you, of course. I organised a DNA test and with that, I was absolved of all responsibility and she is now getting proper help from the state. It was absolutely a gut reaction because I couldn't face another situation like it.'

'Okay, I'm with you so far. Not liking it, but I can accept it. Why did you say you couldn't have children?'

'What? Oh, nothing. I meant I couldn't face it. Not to go through all that again.'

'I see. But what about stealing my car?'

'Laurie had got in with a bad crowd. I mean a really bad crowd. They discovered I was with you and saw us together in your car. They threatened to harm you unless I helped them steal your car. I had to go along with it as I couldn't risk them hurting you. I hated it, but I was so scared I did it. I left the keys out . . . you know the rest. They sold it abroad and got well paid. Laurie didn't see any of the money of course. I left you, coward that I am, because I didn't want you getting involved in all that. I know what they're capable of—they wouldn't have stopped there . . .' His eyes misted over. 'I couldn't risk you being hurt.'

'Surely that's a bit dramatic, isn't it?'

'Maybe, but these guys are on drugs and completely unstable. Who knows what could have happened?'

'That's quite a story. You have no idea what you put me through, Jay.'

'I understand that. I tried to find you again. I went to the Hetherington Hotel but they wouldn't say if you were there or not. I sat outside for over two hours waiting to see if you came in. I gave up eventually and went to stay with my sister. She loaned me some money to buy this van. I might start a catering business or something. I hope you can find it in your heart to forgive me. I do so much want to be a part of our baby's life. If your husband will allow it, of course. I take it you are still going to marry him?'

'What do you think about that?'

'I wish with all my heart that you were marrying me, but I have nothing to offer you. You are used to living in luxury. Oh yes, I have driven past your house a couple of times. It's a huge place. You have every advantage in life. Everything you could want. With me, you'd have to be used to managing with very little money. Rented accommodation at best. I expect Guy has an equally imposing house.'

'But I don't love Guy, whatever sort of home comes with him. He claims to be fond of me but has never used that one word.'

'I love you Georgie. That's precisely why I can never ask you to give up everything for me. I said it before. In time you would resent me, even grow to hate me for what I failed to give you.'

'As long as you promised to love me forever, it is truly all I could want.'

'Really? You mean it?'

'Yes, of course. I've been dreading today. Trying to find an excuse not to marry Guy. I've been living through a nightmare for weeks. Months.'

'And you could actually forgive me for the awful time I put you through?' he asked.

'Mmm. All of that.'

'So what are we going to do?'

'I don't know. Drive away somewhere?'

'Could you do that to your family, Georgie? I don't think so. You have to go back and face them now. Tell them you don't want this marriage. Then you can call me and we will make our plans from there.'

'I'm sure Daddy will never forgive me so it won't be an easy way to a fortune.'

'I'd prefer it that way. I don't want a handout. It will be tough for a while but we can make it if you are absolutely certain.'

'I love you, Jay. That's all that matters to me. I'll go back now before they notice I'm missing. I'll call you later.'

She drove back to her parents' home, a smile on her face that had been missing for many weeks. This was going to be a difficult day but at the end of it, she would be back with the love of her life. Whatever the future held, her beloved Jay was everything she could want.

At midday, when she should have been at the registry office, she called Jay.

'Would you come to the house please, Jay? I have spoken to my parents and they want to meet you.' She sounded determined and calm.

'Are you sure? I mean, is it bad news? Shotguns at dawn?'

She laughed.

'They just want some reassurance that you really do mean what you say about marrying me. I think there's an air of disbelief about the place. I've spoken to Guy and explained.

Naturally, he was very understanding and only a little regretful. I think he was under as much pressure as me to marry.'

'I'll be there in about five minutes. Who will be there?'

'Just my parents and Jenny.'

He arrived at the door looking nervous. Georgie was waiting for him and held his hand as they went into the drawing room. He looked around, trying his best not to look intimidated by the place Georgie called home. Mr Hetherington was looking grim faced but his wife held him back.

'Hello, Jay,' she said quietly. 'Georgie tells me you want be married? She gave us the explanation for your rather erratic behaviour. If she is willing to forgive you, then we cannot object.'

'Mrs Hetherington. Mr Hetherington. First of all, thank you for allowing me to come here. I am truly sorry for the unhappiness I have caused and I would like nothing better than to try and make it up to her. I suppose I should ask formally for her hand in marriage.'

'I don't like it, my boy. None of it. But if it's what she truly wants then she is of age and I can't voice my objections. I'm not promising great financial rewards, or . . .'

'Excuse me interrupting, sir, but I don't want your money. I have little to offer at present but I am a hard worker and very determined to do my best for Georgie and our son.'

'Well said. No more than I would expect. We'd better make arrangements for a wedding very soon. I'll get my secretary onto it and—'

'Thank you, Daddy but no,' Georgie interrupted. 'We plan to go to Poltoon and marry near the beach there.'

'Do we?' Jay asked in surprise.

'Oh yes. We can drive down this afternoon and get married as soon as we can arrange it. You're all welcome to come.'

'I'm not going to interfere any more,' Mr Hetherington announced. 'You clearly have your mind made up. There's one thing to say, Georgina, you seem to have inherited my stubbornness, but I'm proud of the way you've stuck to your guns.' He turned to look at Jay. 'I doubt you'll have an easy time of it with this one, but I'll wish you luck. I'd like to talk to you soon, about your future.'

'I don't want your help, sir. Please be certain of that. I'm marrying Georgie for no other reason than I love her.'

'You've made that very clear. So what do you intend to do?'

'I'd thought of starting a catering service. Ultimately, I'd dream of us being able to run our own hotel. Something small at first, of course.'

'I like your ambition. I might live to regret it one day when you set up in competition.'

219

They were married a week later, not on the beach but after the simple ceremony, they walked on the sand, bracing themselves against the icy blast. Georgie's father had given them an envelope to open later and together, they stared at the cheque with so many noughts on the end that Jay gasped.

'It's enough to actually buy that little hotel in the next village. The one we dreamed of, once upon a time. We can't accept this though, Georgie.'

'Why not? It's a sign that Daddy's forgiven me. Or at least that maybe he sees us as potentially friendly rivals. I love you so much, Jay. You've made me so happy. This is the perfect place to start our lives together and to bring up our son.'